A Winter's Tail
by

Kathi Daley

This book is a work of fiction. Names, characters, places, and incidents either are products of the author's imagination or are used fictitiously. Any resemblance to actual events or locales or persons, living or dead, is entirely coincidental.

I want to thank the very talented Jessica Fischer for the cover art.

I so appreciate Bruce Curran, who is always ready and willing to answer my cyber questions, and Peggy Hyndman for helping sleuth out those pesky typos.

And, of course, thanks to the readers and bloggers in my life, who make doing what I do possible.

Thank you to Randy Ladenheim-Gil for the editing.

Special thanks to Martie Peck, Nancy Farris, Jeannie Daniel, and Vivian Shane for submitting recipes.

And finally I want to thank my sister Christy for always lending an ear and my husband Ken for allowing me time to write by taking care of everything else.

Books by Kathi Daley

Come for the murder, stay for the romance.

Zoe Donovan Cozy Mystery:

Halloween Hijinks
The Trouble With Turkeys
Christmas Crazy
Cupid's Curse
Big Bunny Bump-off
Beach Blanket Barbie
Maui Madness
Derby Divas
Haunted Hamlet
Turkeys, Tuxes, and Tabbies
Christmas Cozy
Alaskan Alliance
Matrimony Meltdown
Soul Surrender
Heavenly Honeymoon
Hopscotch Homicide
Ghostly Graveyard
Santa Sleuth
Shamrock Shenanigans
Kitten Kaboodle
Costume Catastrophe
Candy Cane Caper

Holiday Hangover
Easter Escapade – *April 2017*

Zimmerman Academy The New Normal
Ashton Falls Cozy Cookbook

Tj Jensen Paradise Lake Mysteries by Henery Press

Pumpkins in Paradise
Snowmen in Paradise
Bikinis in Paradise
Christmas in Paradise
Puppies in Paradise
Halloween in Paradise
Treasure in Paradise – *April 2017*
Fireworks in Paradise – *October 2017*

Whales and Tails Cozy Mystery:

Romeow and Juliet
The Mad Catter
Grimm's Furry Tail
Much Ado About Felines
Legend of Tabby Hollow
Cat of Christmas Past
A Tale of Two Tabbies
The Great Catsby
Count Catula
The Cat of Christmas Present

A Winter's Tail
The Taming of the Tabby – *May 2017*

Seacliff High Mystery:
The Secret
The Curse
The Relic
The Conspiracy
The Grudge

Sand and Sea Hawaiian Mystery:
Murder at Dolphin Bay
Murder at Sunrise Beach
Murder at the Witching Hour
Murder at Christmas
Murder at Turtle Cove – *March 2017*

Road to Christmas Romance:
Road to Christmas Past

Writer's Retreat Southern Mystery:
First Case – *May 2017*
Second Look – *July 2017*

Chapter 1

Sunday, February 5

Red and white lights from a sheriff's vehicle flashed on and off, creating a colorful reflection against the dense fog. Tears froze on my cheeks as the darkness beyond the lights closed in around me. The only sound to penetrate the murkiness was a foghorn in the distance, bringing an ominous feel to the tragic scene. As I watched the rescue workers carry the first of the victims up from the depths of the ravine, I prayed that help had arrived in time and this would be a rescue and not a retrieval.

My heart pounded in my chest as the first of the two victims was carried toward the ambulance that was waiting at the side of the road. "Is she...?"

"She's alive." Deputy Ryan Finnegan looked at me with fear evident on his face. "She's lost a lot of blood."

I watched as my best friend in the whole world was lifted into the waiting vehicle. "Can I ride along?"

Finn hesitated.

"Please. I need to be with her."

"Okay," Finn finally answered. "I'll have someone see to your car."

I turned and looked toward the men who were bringing the second body up the steep incline. I glanced at Finn, who only shook his head. I placed my hand over my mouth as a new wave of tears streamed down my face.

"If you're going to go you need to go now," Finn directed as the ambulance technician began to close the door.

I climbed into the waiting vehicle and watched helplessly as the doors closed, blocking the horrific scene that seemed more like a nightmare than reality.

******

I thought the moment I'd seen the car my best friend, Tara O'Brian, was riding in veer away from the oncoming vehicle and go over the side of the steep ravine would be the worst part of this simply horrific day. I was wrong. The worst part was the minutes that clicked by so very slowly as I waited to find out if Tara would live or die.

I'd been told to wait in the reception area of the small island hospital while medical personnel worked to save Tara's life, but waiting, as I'd come to find, was its own kind of purgatory.

After what seemed like a lifetime but was probably only a few minutes, a nurse approached me. "Are you Caitlin Hart?"

"Yes. How is she?"

"Alive." The nurse sat down across from me. "We have her stabilized, and while she's pretty banged up, it appears most of her injuries are fairly minor and should heal over time."

"Most?"

"Your friend has a very deep cut that has caused her to lose a significant amount of blood. We feel it would be best if she had a transfusion. The problem is that she has a rare blood type that we don't have on hand. We could have her airlifted to Seattle, but it would be much better if we can find a donor. Does she have family on the island?"

I struggled to maintain control of my emotions as I momentarily grappled with the secret I'd carried for so long. I knew the secret wasn't mine to tell, but at this moment I knew telling was the only real choice. "Sister Mary. At St. Patrick's Catholic Church. Call Sister Mary."

Siobhan walked in through the double doors leading to the waiting room just after the nurse left to make the call. She opened her arms and I walked into them, knowing that having my big sister on the scene would somehow make everything better. Siobhan's arms tightened around me and she held me for several seconds before asking how Tara was.

"Stable," I answered as she led me over to one of the sofas. "The nurse said the injuries were fairly minor, although she's lost a lot of blood. They recommended a transfusion."

"That doesn't sound so bad," Siobhan tried to comfort me.

"It wouldn't be, except that Tara has a rare blood type. They need to find a donor. I told them to call Sister Mary."

Siobhan frowned, and then a light went on. She was one of only a few people who knew Sister Mary had a daughter. "Tara is Sister Mary's daughter?"

"I think so. I guess we'll know for sure in a few minutes."

The secret that had weighed heavy on my heart for the past two years had first come to light when my boyfriend, Cody West, and I, along with my brother Danny, Tara, and Finn had investigated a cold case concerning the death of Orson

Cobalter, the first owner of the *Madrona Island News*. It turned out Orson had been sitting on details regarding the disappearance of a ten-year-old heiress to millions, the man who had kidnapped her, and the child they had given birth to, for more than twenty-five years. After Orson was murdered we decided to investigate the truth behind the secret, only to discover that Sister Mary was the missing heiress. She had decided at some point to leave behind her life as Maryellen Thornton to begin a life serving God and her community.

"Wow. Finn filled me in on the Maryellen Thornton story after I moved back to the island, but he didn't say anything about Tara being the baby the midwife hid away."

"Finn didn't know the identity of the baby."

"How did you?"

"I didn't. I don't for sure. I had a hunch that seemed to be confirmed by a wink from Tansy," I said, referring to one of two intuits on the island who seem to know everything about everyone but never offer insight beyond a wink or a nod.

"Then it's probably true. Does Sister Mary know what you suspect?"

"No. After we found out she asked the woman who helped her give birth to her daughter to find a good home for her, I guess I naturally began to wonder about the identity of the baby. I knew she still lived in the area, and when I saw the two of them together one day somehow I knew."

"Poor Tara. I'd be willing to bet she has no idea."

Siobhan was right. Tara didn't even know she was adopted, but she had shared with me many times that she felt like an alien in her own family. She got along so well with Sister Mary, who she respected and enjoyed spending time with. I was willing to bet that once the dust settled Tara wouldn't be all that upset to find out her real mother was the woman who already meant so much to her.

Of course, dealing with the fact that her real father was a kidnapper who had impregnated his captive would be another thing entirely.

Siobhan and I didn't have long to discuss the situation before Sister Mary came running into the reception area of the hospital with Father Kilian and my Aunt Maggie on her heels.

I jumped up from my seat and ran to greet the petite woman. I hugged her tight and whispered in her ear, "I'm so sorry. I had to tell."

Sister Mary hugged me in return. "It's okay. You did what you needed to do. I would have done the same thing."

Sister Mary was pulled out of my arms and led down the hall before I had time to respond.

Father Kilian took Maggie by the arm and led her to the seating area. I knew the pair had planned to meet with Sister Mary that afternoon to tell her about his plan to retire and the reason behind it. They still must have been together when Sister Mary received the call from the hospital. It seemed today was destined to be the time for all the secrets I'd been keeping to come crashing out in one giant explosion of truth.

Siobhan led me back to the seating area and we all huddled together as we waited for news. Maggie sat down next to me and took my hand. She gave it a squeeze, as if to convey that everything would be okay. Father Kilian must know the whole truth about Sister Mary, and I could see by the fact that Maggie seemed concerned but not confused that they must have filled her in on the way to the hospital.

"I should call Cody," I said after the waiting had become intolerable. He was in Florida, meeting with members of the SEAL Team regarding the training program he was designing for them. "The cell reception in the hospital is pretty bad, so I'm going to step outside. Someone come get me if the doctor comes out."

I stood up and walked out of the room after the others promised to do just that. I took deep gulps of the cold winter air as I stepped into the light provided by the streetlights lining the drive. I knew it was three hours later in Florida and hoped Cody hadn't gone to bed yet. I needed him tonight more than ever.

"Hey, Cait. I was just about to call you before turning in," Cody said as soon as he answered.

"I have news," I said in a grim tone of voice.

"What?"

"It's Tara. She's been in a car accident."

"Oh God. Is she okay?"

"We're at the hospital. She's lost a lot of blood, but the nurse just told me that other than that her injuries were fairly minor."

I bent down to pet a fluffy white cat that had come over to me as I took a deep breath before letting my mind drift to the events that had led to my standing under a streetlight in front of the hospital on a cold winter's night.

The day had been a strange one from the start. For one thing, my Aunt Maggie had informed me that today, after services, she and Father Kilian planned to have *the talk* with Sister Mary. Father Kilian was going to announce his retirement at services the following week and he wanted Sister Mary to know about it first. Father Kilian wasn't young, and many men his age made the move into retirement without a second thought; what made this announcement so unique was *why* he'd made the decision.

Father Kilian and Aunt Maggie had dated in high school, long before he had become a priest. They'd planned to marry and make a life together, despite the tradition into which Michael Kilian had been born: the oldest son in each generation in his family always entered the priesthood. Just before graduation Maggie had discovered she was pregnant with her boyfriend's baby. Initially the couple were happy even though they knew there would be backlash from both their parents and the church. They were in love and the future seemed full of potential.

The couple's plans were altered drastically when Maggie contracted an infection early on in her pregnancy. She didn't want anyone to find out about the baby so she didn't go to the doctor until it was too late. Aunt Maggie survived, barely, but the baby didn't make it. During the long hours when it had been touch and go for Maggie, Michael had made a deal with God: spare Maggie and he'd enter the priesthood as he seemed destined to do. Maggie returned to her old life, while Michael went off to seminary. Maggie never married and the two remained nothing more than friends for four decades.

Now that it was time for Father Kilian to think about retirement, the couple had begun to wonder if perhaps it was finally their time to have a life together. For them to marry, Father Kilian would have to leave the priesthood entirely. A year ago, he and my aunt had come up with a two-year plan, and now the day had arrived to bring Sister Mary in on their secret. I wondered if she was more surprised by their secret or they by hers. Of course Father Kilian knew part of her story, but I was pretty sure even he didn't know the identity of the baby Sister Mary had given birth to decades before.

Cody promised to come home as soon as he could make the arrangements, and I returned to the waiting room. Siobhan, Maggie, and Father Kilian were there, talking quietly. Other than myself, Siobhan was the only one who knew Maggie's secret before that day, so I thought they might be discussing how the conversation with Sister Mary had gone before they'd rushed to the hospital.

"Any news?" I asked.

"Sister Mary's blood is a match, so they're going ahead with the transfusion," Father Kilian said. "The nurse said a doctor would be out to speak to us in a while."

I sat down between Siobhan and Maggie and prayed Tara would not only recover but would be back to her old self sooner rather than later. I also prayed that the revelation of Sister Mary's secret wouldn't have an adverse effect on either woman. Sister Mary's past had been violent and complicated. Keeping it secret had allowed her to build a new life doing something she loved, but if word got out that she was really Maryellen Thornton the ramifications could be huge.

"What exactly happened?" Maggie asked.

I closed my eyes as the horrific scene played through my mind. I felt like I was watching a video in slow motion. It still didn't seem real.

"We were at Mom's for dinner. The fog rolled in and we decided to head home. There was a car sitting on the side of the road. It was facing north and had its headlights on. As Tanner's car got closer, the vehicle suddenly pulled out onto the road and headed right toward it. Tanner veered to avoid a head-on collision and went over the embankment. It just so happened that the accident occurred at the spot where the road crosses the ravine. If Tanner's car had gone off the road a few seconds earlier or later he simply would have driven into a field. I tried to climb down into the ravine, but the drop off was too steep. Finn came right away, but it was too late."

"And Tanner?" Maggie asked.

"I'm afraid he didn't make it."

Father Kilian immediately began to pray and Maggie started to cry. I didn't know what the next few hours would bring, but I suddenly felt a sense of calm come over me as the cat I had been petting outside the hospital wandered into the waiting area and jumped into my lap.

"Where did you get the cat?" Siobhan asked.

"He was outside when I went to call Cody."

"I'm not sure he should be in here."

I looked around. There was no one to tell me he couldn't stay, so I continued to pet him. I glanced at Father Kilian as he put his arm around Maggie in an attempt, I was sure, to comfort her. On the surface it appeared to be an innocent gesture between priest and parishioner, but knowing what I did, I saw it was so much more.

After what seemed like hours the doctor finally came out to see us.

"My name is Dr. Hamden. I wanted to let you know that Tara is going to be fine. Luckily, Sister Mary was a perfect match and was willing to donate the blood we needed to stabilize her."

"Can I see her?" I asked.

"We've given Tara something to make her sleep. I doubt she'll regain consciousness until tomorrow morning. You should all go home and get some rest."

"And Sister Mary?" I asked.

"We're giving her fluids, but she should be ready to leave shortly." Dr. Hamond turned to go.

I was more exhausted than I could remember ever being before, but I decided to wait with the others for Sister Mary to be released. Besides, I didn't have my car, so I would need a ride home. It wasn't long before Sister Mary was wheeled into the room and Father Kilian left to get his car.

"Thank you," I said once again to Sister Mary.

"Thank you for sending for me. I don't know what I would have done if she hadn't made it."

"I'm so sorry if this presents a problem for you."

"I should be fine." Sister Mary smiled tiredly. "No one asked how it was that I happened to have the same blood type as Tara. There are unrelated individuals with the same blood type, after all. Perhaps they assumed the match was a coincidence—or even a miracle." Sister Mary looked at Maggie, Siobhan, and me. "Despite what has occurred here today, we need to continue to keep the secret. If Maryellen Thornton's family learned she was alive, Tara and I might both be in danger."

I remembered back to the men who had used their knowledge of Sister Mary's identity to blackmail the Thornton family, who very much wanted to make certain Maryellen stayed dead after all these years. She was the heiress to tens of millions of dollars and there were people—extended family—who were better off financially because she was dead. Even if they continued to believe in Maryellen's death, if they found out she had given birth to a child who could be proven to have a claim to her estate, Tara could very well be in the danger Sister Mary alluded to.

"I won't tell," I promised. "But Tara is going to have questions."

Doubt clouded Sister Mary's face. "I'll talk to her. I probably should have before now."

"Why didn't you?"

"I wanted to protect her, but mostly I was frightened. I'm afraid this will be more than she can deal with."

"Tara is a strong woman. She may be shocked at first, but in the end, I think she'll be happy to know."

Sister Mary glanced to the front of the building as Father Kilian came back inside to let us know he'd pulled his car up to the front door. He wheeled Sister Mary out to the vehicle and Siobhan offered to take Maggie and me home. I glanced at the cat standing staring at me with a look of expectation on his face. I picked him up and followed Siobhan to her car. I wasn't sure what the next day would bring, but I knew in my heart that things had changed irrevocably, and tomorrow would bring with it new challenges and a new reality.

Chapter 2

Monday, February 6

I woke to a clear, sunny morning. The fog from the evening before had lifted, and although it was cold, the day looked to be as bright as any we'd had in quite some time. Cody had called first thing to let me know he was wrapping things up with the Navy and would be home on the last ferry that evening. Finn had wanted to interview me regarding the events leading up to the accident the night before, but I'd been so tired by the time he shown up that he'd agreed to come by today to get the information he needed.

The fluffy white cat that had been at the hospital was still with me. I hadn't had time to confirm it with my witchy friend, but I was fairly certain he would turn out to be one of Tansy's magical cats. I leaned down and picked him up and he began to purr.

"So what now?" I asked my feline friend.

The cat batted at my nose.

"If you aren't ready to jump into the investigation I think I might take Max out for a run before Finn shows up."

The cat simply rubbed his head against my shoulder.

"A run it is." I set the cat down on the sofa in front of the fire and then looked at Max, who was lying on the rug there. "Want to go out?"

Max jumped up and headed toward the door.

One of the things I loved best about living on the water was that I could enjoy the ebb and flow of the ocean each morning as I embarked on my morning run. There was something so peaceful about setting a pace to match the rhythm of the tide as seagulls circled overhead and a stray bald eagle swooped down to grab its morning prey. I allowed my mind to focus on the sound of my breath as it mingled with the soft crashing of the waves in the mostly calm sea. I suspected the day ahead would be stressful, so I treasured this last calm moment before the storm.

As I neared Mr. Parsons's place next door, I noticed he was standing on the edge of his property where his lawn met the sand, watching his dog, Rambler, chase the waves. I waved as Max immediately headed in that direction. Cody lived on the third floor of Mr. Parsons's home and most mornings it was Cody who saw to Rambler's run, but with Cody away, the elderly man had had to venture out into the cool morning air.

"Morning, Mr. Parsons," I greeted him.

"Morning, darlin'."

"Have you spoken to Cody today?"

"Yes," he confirmed. "He called last night after he spoke to you. I'm sorry to hear about your friend who passed away. Is Tara going to be okay?"

"She is," I assured him. "She's pretty banged up, but the doctor at the hospital assured us she'll heal over time."

"I spoke to Harland this morning too." Harland Jones was another elderly gentleman who had lived with Mr. Parsons temporarily, after his home had burned to the ground; he'd since found a place of his own and moved out. "He said one of the other residents in the condominium complex had something similar happen last week."

"He was run off the road?"

"He claims he was, although Harland said he admitted he was drunk at the time, and most people assume he passed out and that's why he ended up in the ditch on the side of the road."

"Was he injured?"

"Just a small cut on his forehead."

I made a mental note to ask Finn about the incident. "Do you know the man's name?"

"Last name is Brownly. I think Harland said Kurt Brownly."

I looked at my watch. I really did need to get back. "Thanks for the lead. I'll check it out with Finn. Cody said he'll be home on the last ferry tonight."

"I'll be glad for the company. It's been so quiet since Harland got his own place."

I called Max over to me and we headed back down the beach. I'd just returned from taking my run when my mom called to remind me that I'd promised to go with her to look at a house she was interested in buying. After our family home had burned to the ground the previous summer my mother and youngest sister, Cassidy, had moved into a two-bedroom condo, but Mom liked to entertain and the living area in it was much too small for the family gatherings she hosted every Sunday and on holidays, so she'd been looking for a larger place.

I was assuring her that I would pick her up that afternoon as planned just as Finn pulled up. I went inside the cabin, tossed a log on the fire, and put on some coffee before settling in to answer the questions presented by the man who was not only the island's resident deputy but a lifelong friend and a soon-to-be brother-in-law.

"Cream?" I asked Finn as I poured us both a cup of the hot brew.

"Black is fine."

I poured cream into my own cup and sat down across from him, noting that he held a small tape recorder.

"Okay. What do you want to know?" I asked.

"Start off by telling me your name, age, residence, and relation to the deceased."

I frowned at Finn. "You already know that."

"It's for the record should this end up in court."

"My name is Caitlin Hart, I'm twenty-eight, and I live in a cabin located on my Aunt Maggie's estate on Whale Watch Point on the southwest shore of Madrona Island. The deceased, Tanner Woodson, was a friend."

"And how long had you known Mr. Woodson?"

"About two months. I met him just before Christmas."

"How did you meet?"

"I almost tripped over him on the beach. He'd been assaulted and was lying there unconscious. When he came to he couldn't remember who he was, so my friends and I helped him find out his identity."

"And what were you doing with him on the day he died?"

"He'd come to church and then to my mom's for dinner with my best friend and the other victim of the crash, Tara O'Brian. Do we really need to go into so much detail about things you already know?"

Finn turned off the tape recorder. "No, I guess not. The sheriff seems particularly interested in this case. A deputy from his office showed up this morning to oversee the investigation. I think I might need to do this one by the books."

Finn was referring to the fact that he, Siobhan, Cody, and I often collaborated on local cases. I frowned as I looked out the window at the waves rolling into the shore. "Any particular reason he's so interested?"

"I have no idea, and that worries me. I wish I knew why he was so hyped up about the whole thing."

"It worries you?"

Finn shrugged. "I don't know. Let's just say I have a bad feeling about it. I'd like to get this whole thing wrapped up as soon as possible. Why don't you just tell me what happened that night in your own words?"

Finn turned the recorder back on and I explained into it that I'd been in my car following Tara and Tanner going south on the coast road when a car that had been parked on the other side, heading north, suddenly had pulled into Tanner's lane, causing him to swerve off the road. I also conveyed my opinion that it had seemed to be a deliberate attempt not only to cause the crash but to cause major harm; everything would have ended differently if the car had pulled into Tanner's lane even a fraction of a second earlier or later. "It felt to me like the driver was waiting for Tanner to show up."

"Which would mean that whoever it was would have had to know where Tanner was and when he'd be heading home," Finn pointed out.

I took a deep breath. "But that doesn't make any sense. No one would have known Tanner had gone to Mom's or when he would be going home except those of us who were there."

"For the record, can you state who was present at your mother's condo on the day in question?"

"Just the normal gang, minus Maggie, Marley, and Cody." The normal gang consisted of my mother and Cassidy, my brothers Danny and Aiden, Finn and Siobhan, me and Cody, and, most Sundays, Maggie and her best friend and business partner, Marley Connelly.

I knew Finn probably wanted me to dictate actual names, but he must have taken pity on me because he moved on to the next question.

"Who left the condo before you, Tara, and Tanner?"

"You left with Siobhan right after we ate and Danny left shortly after that. Everyone else was still there when we left to come home."

"And what time was that?"

"I guess around six."

Finn jotted down a few more notes. "Okay, so you were following Tanner's car home and you saw a car parked on the side of the road. Can you describe it?"

I thought for a minute. "Not really. It was foggy, really foggy. The visibility was bad and the headlights from the car were shining in my windshield. I couldn't see anything but the headlights."

"And after the driver of the car ran Tanner off the road? What did he do?"

I paused as I tried to remember. The whole thing had happened so quickly. "He—or I suppose it could have been a she—continued north and disappeared into the fog."

"So the car passed you?"

"Yeah, I guess. After Tanner went off the road I stomped on my brakes. I'd been going only about fifteen miles an hour because the visibility was so bad and I was following at a safe distance, so I was able to stop without too much trouble. The car straightened out and continued north."

"And what did you do at that point?"

"I pulled over to the side of the road and called you. Then I got out and tried to hike down the ravine, but it was too steep and I didn't have a rope or anything."

"Did it seem as if the vehicle that swerved toward Tanner made contact with his car?"

"I don't think so. Tanner went over the side because he overcorrected when he was almost hit by the oncoming car."

Finn took down a few more notes. "Okay, close your eyes. Try to imagine the vehicle passing you. Was it a car? A truck? A van?"

"A car. It was definitely a car."

"Good. Now, was it a large car or a small one?"

I frowned.

"Sedan, sports car, station wagon?"

"It wasn't a large car, but it wasn't small either. I'm going to say it was midsize with two doors. It was loud as it pulled away, which made it seem like a sports car, but it wasn't small like some of them."

"Color?"

"Dark. Maybe black or dark blue. Like I said, it was dark and foggy, so the visibility was minimal. I really can't be sure what color it was."

"Did you notice anything else? Anything at all? Type of wheels, something on the dashboard, bumper stickers, anything?"

I continued to keep my eyes closed as I thought back about what I'd seen. I'd been in shock. I wasn't sure how I even managed to function those first few seconds after Tanner and Tara went over the side of the ravine. It was like I was operating on autopilot. I really had only glimpsed the car as it passed because all my attention had been on the horror in front of me.

"There was music coming from the car," I said. I'd remembered it was loud before, but I hadn't realized why. "Country music, but not modern country music. I'm not a fan of classic country so I don't know the name of the song, but I remember it was loud, with a catchy beat."

"Is it a song you'd heard before?"

"Yeah. It seemed familiar."

Finn took a few more notes before he continued. Of course now that I had a bit of the song in my head I couldn't think of anything else. I hated it when I couldn't remember the name of a tune that echoed in my head over and over again.

"Okay; let's talk motive," Finn moved onto the next subject. "I know you and Tara have spent quite a bit of time with Tanner since he decided to stay on the island after regaining his memory. Did he seem frightened? Distracted? Did he mention any problems in his life?"

"Tara spent more time with him than I had, and I can't think of anything he said that would stand out as indicating fear or concern. He was trying to build a new life and I know there were a few things that weren't exactly going smoothly, but nothing really stands out."

I heard a beep seconds before Finn pulled his phone out of his pocket and looked at it. "I have to go," he informed me. "It looks like I'm going to have a busy day, but I want to continue this discussion. How about if Siobhan and I come by this evening? I'll bring a pizza and we can brainstorm like usual."

"Sounds good to me. Cody will be home on the five-fifteen ferry, so maybe six?"

"Six should be fine. In the meantime, take some notes. Jot down everything you can remember about Tanner: his past and whatever he was working on since his memory returned."

"I will."

Finn turned to leave.

"By the way," I added. "Mr. Parsons told me a man named Kurt Brownly had a similar incident with his car last week. Do you think they could be related?"

"Mr. Brownly was drunk as a skunk when we found him. He did say something about being run off the road, but he wasn't really hurt, and based on his blood alcohol level I figured he'd simply passed out and ended up in the ditch. I doubt the two cases are related. I guess I can have another chat with him, but I doubt I'll learn anything to change my mind about the cause of his accident. On the other hand, while Tanner's accident could have been just that, an accident, it does sound like whoever ran him off the road did so intentionally."

I felt myself tear up for what seemed like the millionth time in the past twelve hours. Tanner had had a rough past and he'd lived a difficult life, but I thought he'd been able to turn a corner. I couldn't imagine why anyone would want to the kill the man we had referred to as John Doe before he'd regained his memory and told us his real name. Poor Tara was going to have a hard time dealing with all this. I knew she was falling for him and had hoped that one day they'd be more than just friends.

I decided to shower and dress and then head into town after Finn left. I wanted to stop by to talk to Tansy about the new feline in my life, and I also wanted to go to the hospital to see if Tara could have visitors. Today was Monday, so the bookstore Tara and I owned was closed, but I'd need to figure out whether I should open tomorrow or if my time would be better spent tracking down the scumbag who had caused this mess in the first place.

Tansy lived and worked with her friend and partner, Bella, in the town of Pelican Bay. The women owned a shop known as Herbalities that specialized in its own brand of herbs, potions, and fortune telling. The shop was a popular place with locals and visitors alike. You could pick up a tea blend to induce tranquility, a salve for your sore muscles, and have your future read all at the same time.

I'd gotten a late start that morning, so I figured they'd already be at their shop by the time I drove to Pelican Bay, so that was where I headed. The sound of chimes greeted me when I opened the front door. Bella was speaking to a customer about the scented candles they sold but paused to indicate that Tansy was expecting me and gestured for me to go on back to the little room where they stored their herbs.

Tansy got up and hugged me as soon as I walked into the room. "I'm so very sorry," she offered as I hugged her back.

"Did you know?" I asked. Tansy had a knack for being aware of things that occurred before anyone else, but I often wondered whether she really could tell the future, as she advertised. She had once handed me a salve for a shoulder injury that hadn't happened yet, which made me curious about why she didn't intervene if she knew something horrible was about to happen.

"Not in the sense you're referring to."

"Could you have stopped it? Warned us?"

"The future is woven on a predestined fabric and isn't mine to manipulate. I'm so very sorry for Tanner, but I sense Tara will be fine."

That was something at least. "And the cat? Did you send him?"

"His name is Moirai. He holds the key to the answers you seek. Trust him and he'll lead you in your search for the truth that lies beyond a shadow of secrecy."

I'd come to learn that Tansy's cryptic messages were meant to be helpful, but at a time like this, when it felt like my world was shattering around me, I really wished she could simply give me the answers I needed with easy-to-understand directions. "Is there anything at all you can tell me? I know you don't like to interfere in the future, but Tanner is dead and my best friend almost died with him." A tear trailed down my cheek. "If you can help please do something."

Tansy took my hand in hers and I could feel a warmth radiate up my arm and into my chest. She looked at me with eyes so dark as to appear almost black. It felt like all my senses had come to life as she stared into the depths of my soul. I wasn't sure what sort of witchy magic she was working, but I suddenly felt my fear and anger dissolve and leave my body, to be replaced by the strength and determination I would need to find the answers I seemed destined to search out.

After a moment Tansy hugged me and stepped away. I felt renewed and regenerated. "Thank you."

Tansy handed me a packet of herbs. "Give these to Tara. They'll aid in her healing. My senses tell me that it will take all the members of your tribe to find the truth within the shadows."

I took the herbs, thanked Tansy again, and left. Truth within the shadows? I had a feeling Moirai, the Scooby Gang, and I were going to have our work cut out for us.

Chapter 3

Tara was sitting up in her bed talking to Danny when I walked into the hospital room carrying a giant balloon and a soft, snuggly stuffed kitty that looked a lot like her cat, Bandit.

"Hi, Danny. I didn't know you were planning to visit," I said to the younger of my two brothers.

He turned and looked at me. "I wanted to see how our girl was doing before I had to leave for my meeting with the guy who's interested in chartering my boat." Danny leaned over and kissed Tara on the forehead before getting up. "I'll stop by again this afternoon."

He and I changed places as he left the small room and I came in and approached the bed. "I brought cheery gifts," I said, trying for a much lighter tone than I was feeling.

"Thank you." Tara tried to smile as I handed her the stuffed cat. "I forgot all about Bandit."

"Don't worry," I reassured her. "I went over to your place to feed him and clean his litter box. I'm going to go back to pick him up on my way home. He can stay with Max, Moirai, and me until his mama gets home."

"Moirai?"

"The cat Tansy sent to help. How are you feeling?"

A tear slid down Tara's cheek. "Physically I'm fine. Other than the cuts and bruises you see, I had a dislocated shoulder that's been reset, but it should heal quickly."

"And mentally?" I asked after carefully sitting down on the edge of the bed and taking her hand in mine.

"Sad. Angry. Scared. Confused. Pick an adjective. At this moment they all seem to work."

"I can see how you might feel that way. How can I help?"

Tara closed her eyes as she sank back against her pillow. Another tear slid down her cheek. "Everything is such a mess. Not only have I been injured in a terrible accident but a man I was beginning to care for has died. I'm sad he's gone, angry at the person who did this, and scared that he or she was really after me and will try again when I get out of here."

I frowned. "Why would anyone be after you?"

Tara opened her eyes and looked at me. "Why would anyone be after Tanner?"

I took a deep breath and considered my response. "I don't know why anyone would want Tanner dead. The men who were after him last December are either dead or behind bars, so I doubt this incident is related. And I agree he seemed to be a sweet, gentle guy, but that doesn't mean he didn't have secrets we were unaware of."

Tara wiped the tears from her face with the back of her hand. I handed her a tissue from the box on the nearby table.

"I guess that's true," she admitted. "Still, we need to figure out who did this."

"And we will," I promised.

"Every time I think of how senseless this whole thing is I want to scream at the world and demand retribution, but then I remember the sweet, gentle man I was beginning to love and know he wouldn't want me out in the world seeking vengeance." Tara closed her eyes, then, after several seconds, reopened them. "Did you know? Did you know about Sister Mary?"

"I suspected," I admitted.

"Why didn't you tell me?"

"She didn't want anyone to know, including you. I don't think she wanted to mess up your life or the relationship you have with your mom. Did she come to talk to you about things?"

"Yeah. First thing this morning. She didn't want me to figure it out on my own. To be honest, the way my head is still spinning I doubt I would have. At least not right away. She explained everything and then she told me you knew somehow and you were the one who told them to call her to the hospital. I should thank you for that."

"You don't have to thank me. I'm your best friend. A best friend's job is to keep your secrets until they need to be told and then tell them."

Tara smiled weakly and closed her eyes again.

"So how do you feel about the fact that Sister Mary is your birth mother?"

"Like I said before, my emotions are all over the map. I'm confused because I'm not sure what it will mean for the rest of my life. Sister Mary wants us to continue to keep her secret. She feels it's the safest course of action, and I guess I agree. But I'm scared things between us will change. We've always had such a special relationship and I would hate it if everything got awkward." Tara took a deep breath. "But most of all, I'm happy.

I'm happy I finally understand why I've always felt like an alien in my family and I have a newfound love for my mom for taking me in and raising me, even though she had no idea where I'd come from. And, despite my fears, I'm excited to explore a new relationship with a woman who's always felt like a mother to me." Tara glanced at the brown bag I still held. "What's in that?"

"Herbs from Tansy. She said they'll help you heal."

"Then hand them on over. I can't begin to tell you how much I want to get out of this hospital."

"When you do get out come and stay with me. You shouldn't be alone."

"Thanks. I'd like that. I'm going to talk to Dr. Hamden to see if he'll let me go home today. The nurse seemed doubtful, but this place is so depressing and I really am okay. I just need time to heal and I can do that just as well at your place."

I placed my hand on Tara's arm. "If you can talk the doctor into springing you call me and I'll come right back to get you."

"Thank you. You're a good friend."

After I left the hospital I headed home to find my kitty houseguest had knocked most of the things that had been on the kitchen counter onto the floor.

"Moirai," I complained, "what's with the mess?"

He watched as I picked everything up. When things were back the way I'd had them, he jumped back onto the counter and began batting books and paper onto the floor again.

"Stop," I demanded. I looked at the cat, who stood staring at me. "It seems you're trying to get my attention, which you have, so what is it you want?"

Moirai leaped down and went over to the door.

"You want to go somewhere?"

"Meow."

"Okay, where?"

He trotted over to the papers he'd scattered on the floor and sat on top of one of them. I bent over and he moved so I could pick it up. It was an old newspaper I'd picked up when Tara and I were helping Tanner find a more permanent place to live than the house he'd initially rented.

"You think we should go over to Tanner's place?"

"Meow." Moirai ran to the door once again.

"Okay, but we'll need to be quick. I'm supposed to pick up my mom in a couple of hours and I need to call Finn before that. I've been thinking about the fact that the man who ran Tanner and Tara off the road happened to be in the right place at the exact right time. The only explanation I can come up with is that he was following Tanner. Maybe he was tracking his phone or there was a tracker on the car."

"Meow."

"So you agree? I'll just be a minute and then we can head over to Tanner's place."

I called Finn and brought up the tracking idea. He agreed it had merit and promised to look into it. He also told me that the deputy the sheriff had assigned to head up the investigation would most likely want to speak to me. He reminded me that I needed to answer honestly but also be careful what I said because everything, he assured me, would be part of the public record.

I hung up with Finn, grabbed a cat carrier from the Harthaven Cat Sanctuary, which was located on the grounds of the estate where I lived, and headed toward Pelican Bay for the second time that day. Tanner had planned to open a restaurant with the help of his ex-brother-in-law and had been renting a small, one-bedroom apartment which he'd recently moved into while he scouted the island for a location. I didn't have a key to the apartment, but I knew the landlady. Hopefully she'd let my kitty sidekick and me inside for a few minutes.

It turned out the door was unlocked, so I slipped in with Moirai while Max waited in the car.

"What do you think?" I asked as I looked around the sparsely furnished apartment. I had no idea why Moirai had wanted to come to the apartment, so I figured I'd just follow his lead.

I noticed Tanner had left a photo of Tara on the table next to the landline. In and of itself, the fact that Tanner had a photo of the woman he was casually dating wasn't odd, but the placement of the photo near the phone, along with a handwritten note that listed five names gave me pause. Two of the names were followed by what looked to be phone numbers. I picked up both the photo and the piece of paper and stashed them in my backpack.

I looked around for Moirai, who had wandered into the kitchen. I frowned when I noticed an empty glass and a half-full bottle of scotch on the counter. Tanner was a recovering alcoholic who had promised both Tara and his ex-brother-in-law he was sober and could be trusted and depended on. Perhaps he wasn't doing as well as he'd led everyone to believe.

"Is this what you wanted me to see? That Tanner had been drinking again?"

"Meow."

I thought back a couple of months, to the first time I had seen Tanner. He had tried to commit suicide and ended up half-dead on the beach after witnessing a murder outside a bar. It occurred to me that Tanner should never have been hanging out in that bar in the first place, and now there was evidence he was still drinking. Maybe he wasn't as committed to his sobriety as he wanted everyone to believe.

Moirai led me into the bedroom, then crawled under the bed. I got down on the floor and looked underneath. The space was empty except for a small box that looked like the tackle boxes fishermen used to store their gear. I pulled it out and opened it. Sure enough, it was filled with lures, hooks, and other fishing supplies. The box was a lot like the ones Aunt Maggie sold at the Bait and Stitch. On the surface its presence in the apartment didn't present any red flags, but I'd known

Tanner for almost two months and not once had he mentioned going fishing. I'd have to ask Tara about that. She'd spent a lot more time with him than I had.

I was about to slide the box back under the bed, but Moirai had led me to it, so perhaps there was something to find that wasn't immediately evident. I picked it up and looked at the cat. "I have the tackle box and the note by the phone. Anything else?"

He trotted over to the front door and sat down. It appeared I had found what Moirai wanted me to after all. I considered locking the door on my way out but remembered the other deputy in town and decided to leave things exactly the way I'd found them. Moirai and I returned to the car and I considered what to do next as I started the engine. There had been five names on the list next to the phone: Darby, Colton, Stuart, Ray, and Bosley. The first two names were followed by a number with seven digits. My money was on them being phone numbers. I didn't know for certain who the five people listed were, although a man named Colton Banner was the owner of Shots, an island bar. Tanner had been there when he'd witnessed a man named Turner Carson shoot and kill Bruce Drysdale. Carson was in jail now, and as far as I knew, Tanner hadn't been back to Shots, but if the Colton on the list was the owner of the bar, maybe Tanner had been hanging out there again.

I called the number next to Colton's name to test my theory that the seven digits were phone numbers. It was confirmed when the phone was answered by an answering machine that informed callers of the bar's hours of operation. Shots wouldn't be open until later in the afternoon, so I called Danny, who was a frequent bar patron himself, and asked him if he had a way to get hold of Banner.

"What's up?" Danny asked after one ring.

"I wondered if you knew how to get hold of Colton Banner."

"What do you want with him?"

"I found his name on a list in Tanner's apartment and decided to follow up to see if he had any insight into Tanner's activities in the days before the accident."

"Colton had some medical issues a while back and decided to clean up his act. He's been in rehab for at least a month. I doubt he's talked to Tanner since he left the island, although I did hear he was planning to sell the bar and I know Tanner was looking for a place to open his restaurant."

"Shots isn't a restaurant," I pointed out.

"No, but it does have a small kitchen and there'd be adequate space to convert that area. It would take a load of money to turn the place into the sort of fine-dining establishment Tanner has been talking about, but his brother-in-law is loaded. Listen, I have to go. The guy who's leasing my boat is on his way over to get the keys."

"So the deal you were hoping to make worked out?"

"It did. The guy wants to lease the boat through May, which will help my cash flow significantly. The only downside is that I have to move out, but Maggie said I could crash at her place. Is the gang getting together tonight?"

"Finn mentioned something about coming by at around six."

"You cooking?"

"I think pizza was mentioned."

"Perfect. I'll be by. I really would like to find whoever did this to Tara. Hey, the guy I'm waiting for just pulled up. I'll talk to you later."

I frowned at Moirai after I hung up the phone. I doubted I'd be able to talk to

Banner if he was in rehab, though I supposed I could still stop by to chat with whoever was in charge once the bar opened. In the meantime I needed to pick up Bandit and drop him at the cabin along with Moirai and Max before picking up my mother. I wasn't sure why she'd picked me of all her children to help her with this task, but she didn't often ask me to be a part of the important decisions in her life, so I was happy to oblige her.

******

"So, tell me about this house," I said as we drove from her condo toward the sea.

"It's located in old Harthaven, less than a block from the water. It has three bedrooms, two and a half bathrooms, and a large living area with an open floor plan. I'm really anxious to see it. The photos I saw made it look perfect and Aiden said it's within my budget."

My oldest brother, Aiden, had been taking care of my mother's finances ever since my father had passed away.

"I'm surprised you didn't ask Aiden to come with you to look at the house."

"If I decide I'm interested in making an offer I'll have him take a look, of course, but you know Aiden uses logic to approach most situations. He wouldn't even notice the crown molding or the delightful breakfast nook with a partial view of the water. All he'd be interested in would be how much we would need to offer and if the terms were to his liking."

"I guess you have a point, and Danny probably wouldn't be much better. Although I'm surprised you didn't wait to see it until Cassie could come along. She'll be living in the house with you after all."

"I wanted to look at the house today and the only available time for a showing was two o'clock. Cassie doesn't get out of school until three-thirty. Besides, I wanted to spend some time with my middle daughter. You've been so busy lately, I never see you."

"I come to dinner almost every Sunday," I said as I turned into the older yet well-kept neighborhood.

"Sunday's don't count." Mom took out a piece of paper. She unfolded it and then looked out the window. "It should be on the right side. According to the photo, the house is blue-gray with white trim."

"I think I see it." I began to slow down as we approached a property with a sign in the front that said "For Sale by Owner."

"It's nice," I said as I pulled up to the curb. "I love the dormers and the paint looks new."

"It does have a lot of nice features." Mom smiled. "The owner should be here to show us around, so let's go on up."

The yard was nicely groomed, and although it was winter, I could see that during the spring the bushes and shrubs would be bright with colorful flowers. There was a covered porch that looked like it wrapped at least halfway around the two-story house, bringing a cozy feel to the property. The porch swing, which had been newly painted to match the house, rocked gently in the breeze, reminding me of one my grandmother had had when I was growing up.

Mom knocked on the door. We didn't have to wait long before a nice-looking man I imagined was about my mother's age opened the door.

"Mrs. Hart?" he inquired.

"I'm Martha Hart and this is my daughter Caitlin."

He stepped aside. "My name is Gabe Williams. Please come in."

The house was open and airy, with a ton of windows that seemed to merge the interior with the lush landscaping outside. I could see a small peek of ocean through the window of the main living area, which was nice, but I thought the view from the second story would be fantastic.

"Your home is gorgeous," I commented. "So open and spacious, and I absolutely love the hardwood floors."

"Thank you. The place was pretty run down when we first purchased it, but after close to nine years of blood, sweat, and tears, I think we created something to be proud of."

"You really have." Mom walked over to look out the window. "It's very cozy and homey. Do you mind if I ask why you're selling?"

"My wife died eighteen months ago. It was a hard decision, but the house is really too much for just one person. My daughter has been bugging me for over a year to downsize and she finally managed to wear me down."

"Does your daughter live with you?" Mom asked.

"No. She's a doctor and lives in Portland." Gabe turned and glanced at me. "Does your daughter live with you?"

"No, Cait has her own place. My youngest daughter, Cassidy, lives with me. She's still in high school. We also decided to downsize after our family home burned down, but trust me, small spaces aren't the attraction they might seem."

"So it's just the two of you?"

"Yes. My dear husband has been gone for going on six years now."

I couldn't help but notice the interest in his eyes. I had a feeling that if Mom played her cards right she might come out of this deal with more than just a fabulous new house.

Chapter 4

We took a leisurely tour of the house and then I dropped Mom back at home and headed toward Shots. As charming as Gabe seemed to be, and as much fun as I'd had exploring his house with my mother, I couldn't help but feel I should be working on tracking down the lowlife who had almost killed my best friend instead of discussing window coverings. The only clues I had at this point were the five names on the list I'd found at Tanner's place, and the only one I'd been able to possibly identify was that of Colton Banner. Just one of the remaining four had been followed by a seven-digit number. I'd tried calling the number associated with Stuart, but it just rang and rang.

Shots was located on the far west end of Pelican Bay, a drinker's bar that specialized in generous shots of top-quality hard liquor. It tended to attract a late-night crowd, so in the afternoon it was conveniently all but deserted. I walked up to the bar and ordered a diet cola.

"Don't have soda," the bartender informed me.

"That's right; I remember that from last time. I really just wanted to ask you about Tanner Woodson. Did you know him?"

"Yeah, he came around, or at least he did. Heard he was in a car accident."

"I understand he might had been speaking with Colton Banner about buying this place."

The bartender frowned. "I don't know anything about that. As far as I know, Colt plans to keep it."

"Tanner had written down the bar's phone number with Colton's name and I was curious as to what they might have talked about. A friend told me Colton was in rehab and might want to sell."

"This'll be the ninth or tenth time Colt has done the rehab thing. I doubt he's looking to sell. He makes a good living with this bar without working all that hard."

"Can you think of any other reason Tanner might have written down the bar's number?"

The bartender shrugged. "No idea. Now if you don't mind, I have to get set up before the happy-hour crowd begins to arrive."

I left the bar and sat in my car wondering what to do next. I'd hoped to have something relevant to share at the Scooby meeting that night, but other than the fact that Mom might very well have found a new friend, I was coming up dry. I thought about calling Finn to find out if he'd made any headway with the five names I'd given him, but he'd asked me to keep a low profile while the deputy the sheriff had sent was in town, so the least I could do was honor his request.

I was about to head home when I received a text from Siobhan asking me to stop by her office. It wasn't all that much out of my way, so I returned the text, letting her know I'd be there within ten minutes.

When I arrived I saw Aiden was there too.

"What's up?" I asked my two oldest siblings as I took a seat at the conference table where they were sitting.

"Mom called Aiden about ten minutes before I texted you to tell him she wanted to make an offer on the house the two of you looked at. Aiden reminded her that she'd just started looking and it would be best to get a broader view of what was out there before making an offer, but she was insistent. That seems fast even for Mom, who has demonstrated a propensity to be somewhat spontaneous and reactive lately. We knew you'd gone to look at the house with her and hoped you could fill us in."

I knew Mom had been charmed by Gabe Williams and he by her the minute they laid eyes on each other. She must have called Aiden as soon as I dropped her off at her house.

"The house is very nice," I began. "It's newly remodeled and in excellent shape. The views from the second floor are matched only by homes actually on the water, and the garden, which is dormant now, will be exactly the sort of thing that would occupy Mom for hours on end come spring."

"It does sound nice," Siobhan admitted.

"It is. The kitchen is large, with new appliances, and the dining and living area are open to each other, which gives the downstairs a larger feel than the square footage would indicate."

Siobhan glanced at Aiden, who had yet to speak. "I guess it wouldn't hurt to take a look at the place," she said.

"Oh, I think you definitely should. And while you're there, be sure to introduce yourself to Gabe."

"Gabe?" Siobhan asked.

"The man who's selling the house was persuaded to put the place on the market because his daughter thinks it's too much for him since his wife passed away. I could see he loves it and is reluctant to let it go."

"So he'll probably back out even if Mom does make a good offer," Siobhan suggested.

"Maybe. But the minute Mom and Gabe met I could feel the spark between them. He's very sweet and very good-looking, and it's obvious he was totally devoted to his wife. The home they created from a run-down house was truly a labor of love."

"I'd like to meet him and see the house," Siobhan said.

"Call him. He mentioned he had some other showings and would be around all afternoon. I'm sure he'd be happy to meet both of you."

I glanced at my phone and saw I had a text from Tara. "I have to go. It looks like Tara has somehow managed to talk Dr. Hamden into releasing her from the hospital provided she has someone to take care of her."

"That's good news," Siobhan said.

"It is." I texted back to let Tara know I was on my way.

"Do you have any news about the accident?" Siobhan asked.

"I found a piece of paper with five first names on it in Tanner's house. I'm trying to track down the people behind the names. Unless something changes, we're planning to meet tonight to go over what we do know."

"I'll bring the murder board," Siobhan volunteered.

"And I'll bring the wine."

Aiden rolled his eyes but didn't say anything more.

As I drove to the hospital, I decided to set Tara up in Cody's spare room. My place was so tiny and the only sleeping areas were the loft and the sofa, but Cody had two very comfortable bedrooms and he was always hoping we'd spend more time at his place. He'd even remodeled it to make me feel more comfortable. At first I'd been hesitant to have him change his bachelor pad into more of a couple's retreat, but I assumed we would live there together one day and I thought he'd wanted to give me a chance to get used to the place.

I had a chat with the doctor as soon as I arrived at the hospital, and he gave me a fistful of medications and instructions regarding my patient. I promised to follow every instruction to the letter before thanking him for saving my friend's life and heading down the hall to rescue her.

"I'm so glad you're here." Tara was already dressed and sitting in a wheelchair. "I can't wait to get out of here. This place is making me nuts."

"Where did you get the clothes?" I paused, noticing that she was wearing fresh clothes, not the bloody ones she'd had on when she was brought in the previous evening.

"I had Danny stop by my place to get them when he visited earlier. I would have just had him pick me up now, but he was heading to his boat to get the last of his stuff before the man who leased it headed south."

"Is something wrong with your legs?" I nodded toward the wheelchair.

"My legs are fine. Wheeling me out is some sort of rule. I'm supposed to wait for the nurse, who should be here any minute."

I shrugged and sat on the edge of the bed. "You seem better."

"I am, thanks to you."

Except for the fact that she looked like she'd been in a boxing match, had stitches in her side, and sported a nifty-looking sling, Tara almost looked like her old self.

"Any news about the lowlife who did this?" Tara asked.

"Not yet, but I'm working on it. The gang will be coming by to work on it this evening."

"Good. We need to catch this guy before he gets away. Tanner was a good guy who didn't deserve to die in such a needless way. The man or woman responsible has to pay for what they did."

"And they will."

We paused our conversation when the nurse walked in with Tara's release paperwork.

I got her settled at Cody's place, then asked my neighbor, Francine Rivers, to stay with her while I went back to my cabin to pick up some overnight things and called Siobhan to let her know we were moving our get-together that evening. She was on her way to see Gabe Williams's house but offered to call everyone to let them know we'd be meeting at Cody's once she had finished there.

At my cabin, I decided I'd take Max, Bandit, and Moirai over to Cody's place too because we'd be spending most of our time there now that Tara was staying with us. I packed everything I thought I'd need and then went up to the big house to fill Maggie in on what was going on.

"Maggie, are you here?" I called as I entered through the back door.

"Upstairs in the sewing room."

I jogged up the stairs and down the hall. "What a beautiful dress. Is it for the ball?" I asked. The island held a formal ball every Valentine's Day, though most years Maggie didn't attend.

"It is for the ball, but it isn't for me. One of the women from the garden club asked me if I would alter it for her. It used to belong to her cousin, who no longer wanted it, but it needed to be shortened and let out a bit. How's Tara?"

"Better. She'll be staying at Cody's because he has an extra bedroom. I'll be staying there as well, which is what I came over to tell you."

"I'm glad she's doing better. Let me know if there's anything I can do."

"I will. By the way, I've been wondering how your talk with Sister Mary went. Before you were interrupted, of course."

Maggie set her sewing aside and looked at me. "Better than I even hoped. She seemed to understand the situation

Michael and I found ourselves in and appears to be supportive of our plans. I can't tell you what a relief it was that she wasn't angry or upset. I've been keeping this secret for so long, I guess I built up the worst-case scenario in my mind."

"I'm glad things went well." I paused. "And I know the secret still needs to be kept, but I was wondering if I could tell Cody. It feels wrong to keep something so big from him, even if it isn't my secret I'm keeping, and I know Siobhan would like to tell Finn as well."

Maggie hesitated before answering. "I'm sure you're aware that there are some parts of the secret that will be revealed over time and others that won't ever be revealed. I trust both Finn and Cody, and it isn't fair of me to ask you to keep it from the men you plan to build your lives with, so I'm fine with you girls sharing the details with them, but only them."

I let out a sigh of relief. Keeping so many secrets from Cody had been weighing on my mind more than I'd realized.

By the time I returned to Cody's third-floor apartment the Scooby Gang had begun to assemble. Siobhan and Tara were chatting with Danny, who'd arrived while I'd been gone. Siobhan broke away from the others and pulled me aside the minute I walked through the door.

"I love the house and I love Gabe," Siobhan shared. "I have to admit that when we were talking in my office I was worried Mom might be jumping into another chancy relationship, but I can totally understand what you see in him. I wish I could have been there when Mom was, to see how they interacted."

"I'm sure it won't be long before Mom is calling us all together to introduce us to him." I suddenly cringed when I remembered the last man she'd introduced us to. What a difference! "What did Aiden say?"

"He wasn't quite as charmed. When he dropped me off at my office after we visited with Gabe he was mumbling something about having Finn do a background check on him, which actually would be a good idea."

"I agree, but my gut tells me that he won't find anything. If I had to guess I would say Mom and Gabe might have a future together."

"Do you think Mom thinks so?" Siobhan asked.

Good question. "I don't think she's picking out a wedding dress just yet, but I could tell she was attracted to Gabe. If I was a betting woman, I'd say one of them calls the other for some reason or another before too much time passes. And Mom does want to make an offer on the house. Aiden won't be able to put her off for too long."

"Cassie hasn't even seen the house yet."

"True. And after what happened the last time I would assume Mom would make sure Cassie was totally comfortable with everything that happens."

"She may not be thrilled if Mom has found a new guy."

"Maybe not."

Siobhan's phone rang just as Cody was pulling up, so I went outside to greet him. He hadn't been gone all that, long but it had felt like an eternity. What he was doing was important, but I would be glad when his project came to an end.

"I was hoping to get home before the crowd assembled," Cody whispered in my ear after pulling me aside and planting a hello kiss on me. "I've missed you."

"I've missed you too. Don't worry; once everyone leaves and Tara turns in for the night we'll find some alone time."

"Is everyone here?"

"Finn is on his way."

"Is there food? I'm starving."

"Danny brought beer, wine, and soda and Finn is picking up pizza after he grabs Siobhan's white board."

"Is there anything I should know before we go in?"

"Not really. I've had a nonstop day, but I don't have much to base an investigation on. I do have a list of names, though, so maybe one of them will mean something to someone in the group."

"Don't worry; we'll figure this out."

"I know. We always do."

I laced my fingers through Cody's as we entered the house through the back entrance. Everyone was talking, so no one noticed our arrival.

"I take it the new cat sitting on Danny's lap is a Tansy cat," Cody said.

"His name is Moirai and he found me at the hospital. So far he hasn't been a ton of help, but we're just getting started."

Cody squeezed my hand. "It looks like we have a few minutes. I'm going to head downstairs to say hi to Mr. Parsons. I won't be long. I'd wait until after, but we never know how long these meetings might go on and I want him to know I'm home."

"Okay. If Finn shows up before you get back I'll text you."

Cody kissed me and then headed down the back steps. I continued into the room and joined the conversation.

"Did I just see Cody?" Danny asked.

"He went to say hi to Mr. Parsons. He won't be long."

"We were just talking about the list," Siobhan offered. "I know we don't have much at this point, but I think that in the long run it might prove to be of real value. I just wish there were last names. Some of these first names are pretty common. I don't know how we'll narrow them down."

"We need to figure out where Tanner might have come into contact with people bearing these names." I looked at Tara. "He didn't have a job. Do you know how he spent his time?"

Tara frowned. "When we were together we hung out at my place, looked at properties for the restaurant he wanted to open, and occasionally had dinner." She paused and looked off into the distance. "I'm not sure what he did all day while we were at work. He never mentioned it and I never asked. At the time it didn't seem odd, but now that you mention it, it does seem strange it never came up."

"We should have Finn check credit card statements," Siobhan suggested. "Knowing where he spent his money will tell us what he was doing with at least part of his time."

Siobhan looked out the window. "Finn's here. Maybe he has news."

Chapter 5

What Finn had to tell us was both shocking and confusing, to say the least.

"Another victim?" I asked.

"Same MO. The car was run off the road by a dark-colored sedan approaching head on. The driver, a man named Stuart Evans, is being airlifted to Seattle. The EMTs aren't sure whether he'll make it or not."

"If Evans was injured that badly how do you know about the other car?" I asked.

"He was in bad shape, but he didn't lose consciousness immediately. He managed to call 911 himself and told the operator that the other vehicle veered into his lane and ran him off the road. He gave his location to the operator, but by the time the rescue workers got there he was out cold and hasn't regained consciousness since."

I frowned. "You said Stuart? Stuart is one of the five names on the list I found in

Tanner's apartment." I took a few minutes to explain to Cody and Tara that I'd gone by Tanner's house and found the list with the names and numbers on it while Siobhan found a stack of plates and napkins.

"So what does that mean?" Tara asked.

"I don't know," I admitted. "Maybe nothing. Maybe the Stuart who was run off the road isn't even the Stuart on the list."

"It seems like we should figure out a way to find out for sure," Siobhan said.

"There was a phone number next to the name Stuart on the list. I've tried calling it several times, but it just rings and rings," I told them. "Finn, can't you find out who the number belongs to? That will tell us if we're dealing with the same person."

"Give me the number again and I'll find out right now," Finn said.

I read off the number while everyone helped themselves to a slice of the pizza. I could tell by the frown on Finn's face that he wasn't happy with the answer he'd received to his inquiry.

"The number is associated with a burner cell. I'll do some more checking to see if I can figure out who bought it and when."

"So do you think Tanner and Stuart were targeted, or is some lunatic driving around randomly running people off the road?" Tara asked.

"I'm not sure," Finn admitted. "I think at this point we should treat the attacks as targeted, not random. If the Stuart in this accident is the same one on Tanner's list, we might be able to find a link fairly easily. If not, we have a tough job ahead of us."

"Let's finish eating and then we'll use the murder board to begin to build a theory," Siobhan suggested. "We'll need to find out everything we can about today's victim whether he's Tanner's Stuart or not." Siobhan looked at Cody. "Do you have a computer we can use?"

"My laptop is still in my truck. I'll get it after we eat."

"Has Tanner's family been notified?" Tara asked Finn.

Finn set down his slice of pizza and turned to Tara. "I called Anthony Princeton, Tanner's ex-brother-in-law, because he was the only person I knew of. He was, of course, saddened by the news, though he didn't seem overly distraught. In fact, I thought his entire demeanor seemed off. I decided to ask a few more questions."

"And…?" Tara asked.

"And the story Tanner told us and the one Princeton told me on the phone today don't totally line up."

Tara placed her hand on her forehead and rubbed the knot she'd received in the accident the night before. "What do you mean?"

Finn glanced at Siobhan, who had finished her piece of pizza and was beginning to organize the murder board. He took a couple of quick bites of his own slice, then washed it down with the beer Danny had handed him. Then he opened the file folder he'd brought in with him and took out a typewritten report. "When Tanner regained his memory last Christmas, he told us that prior to running into his estranged wife's brother he'd been a broke, homeless man living on the street. He said his brother-in-law had given him money for a place to stay as well as an opportunity for a new start if he cleaned himself up. Tanner told us he knew he needed to get his life together, so he took advantage of Princeton's help and did just that. At some point Princeton arranged for Tanner to come to Madrona Island, where he was to meet his wife and daughter."

Everyone waited expectantly while Finn paused to take a breath.

"According to my notes," he continued, "Tanner said he arrived on the island on December 8. His wife and daughter were due to arrive on the midday ferry on Sunday, December 11. When he arrived at the terminal just as the ferry was pulling up to the dock a man who worked on the car deck handed him a letter he claimed had been given to him by a woman at the port at Anacortes."

"That was the letter from his wife that we found in the house he was renting," Tara said. "The letter asking for a divorce."

"Yes," Finn confirmed. "When I spoke to Princeton today his story started off the same as Tanner's. He said he'd run into Tanner, who appeared to be living on a park bench. He felt bad for him and partially responsible for the mess Tanner was in, so he gave him money and encouraged him to clean himself up. Initially, it appeared as if Tanner was following his advice, so he agreed to try to arrange a visit with his sister. He didn't specify exactly how he found out Tanner had started drinking again, but when he realized he wasn't in recovery, as he thought, Princeton was the one to encourage his sister to cancel her visit, which she'd done well before December

11. When Tanner called him to complain that he'd interfered in a matter that was between him and his wife, Princeton told Tanner that his sobriety was a nonnegotiable condition of the arrangement they had come to, and because Tanner hadn't kept up his end of the bargain he was no longer willing to help him financially. Princeton went as far as encouraging his sister to end her relationship with Tanner completely."

"Wait," Tara spoke up. "If Tanner's brother-in-law wasn't helping him how was he going to buy his own restaurant? We'd been looking for a location for a month."

"According to Princeton, he had no intention of buying a restaurant for Tanner. He said Tanner knew that, so he had no idea why he was continuing to look for a location."

Tara placed her hand on her heart, which I knew must be breaking. I hoped she would manage to get through this whole thing unscathed. Tara had a huge heart and a wonderful ability to see the good in people. I hoped this wouldn't taint her outlook on life. "Maybe Princeton is wrong. Maybe Tanner hadn't fallen off the wagon. We've been dating casually for over two months and I haven't seen him take a single drink."

"There was a half-empty scotch bottle on his kitchen counter when I went to his apartment today," I said. "When I spoke to the bartender at Shots he said Tanner was a frequent customer. And the bar's phone number was on Tanner's list, next to the name Colton. Colton Banner owns Shots, who, coincidentally," I added, turning to Danny, "*is* in rehab."

"And Tanner did say the murder he'd witnessed just before losing his memory took place outside Shots," Cody added.

"So he's been lying to me this whole time?" A single tear slid down Tara's cheek.

"I think so," Finn answered with compassion in his voice. "We found a flask in his jacket pocket when we recovered his body, so we checked his blood alcohol level. Tanner was legally drunk at the time of the accident."

"He didn't seem drunk," Tara argued.

"People who drink a lot have coping mechanisms to hide their addiction. It isn't surprising you didn't realize," Danny offered with sympathy in his voice.

"Okay, so what does this all mean?" Siobhan asked. She turned to look at me.

I didn't answer, and neither did anyone else.

"Are we sure, now, that the accident Tanner and Tara were in wasn't simply that?" Danny asked. "If he'd been drinking maybe he misjudged the oncoming car and that's why they ended up in the ravine."

"No," I stated firmly. "I was right behind them. I saw the other car swerve into their lane. The fact that it had been parked on the side of the road and seemed to head right for them looked intentional to me."

"Besides, we have two separate accidents now," Siobhan pointed out. "I doubt both Tanner and Stuart Evans just misread the situation. I'm going to start two columns on the murder board, one for Tanner and one for Evans. We'll list everything we can think of and maybe we'll find a link. Chances are whoever was driving that other car had a reason to want both of them dead."

"There's a guy named Stuart who works over at the Harthaven Marina," Danny said suddenly. "Or at least he did over the summer. I'm not sure he's been around since they laid off the seasonal staff."

"Do you know him?" I asked.

"Not really, but I know who he is. He's new to the island. I'm pretty sure he first showed up here last summer. If we want to dig up the lowdown on him the marina is a good place to start. I can head over there tomorrow and put out some feelers."

"I'll go with you," I offered. "I'm not sure what the link between Tanner and this Stuart could be—Tanner didn't have a boat and most likely never hung out at the marina—but unless the accidents really were random, there must be a connection."

"Maybe; maybe not," Finn cautioned. "It's possible the sedan driver chose his victims randomly, based on opportunity. Stranger things have happened."

I disagreed. "Maybe in a city, but not on Madrona Island."

"Just because we're a small community doesn't mean we're immune from emotionally disturbed individuals," Finn countered. "If the Stuart on Tanner's list turns out to be the same person who was in the second accident maybe we can rule out a random act. Until we can determine it, though, I think we should at least consider the possibility."

"You said there were five names on the list you took from Tanner's apartment.

Who were the other three?" Siobhan asked.

"Bosley, Ray, and Darby."

Siobhan wrote down the names. "Were there phone numbers with them?"

"No. Just the first two names," I answered.

"The name Bosley seems familiar, but I can't quite place it. There was a guy named Darby Prater who bowled in the same league I used to belong to," Finn offered. "I'll call him to see if he knew Tanner. Darby isn't a real common name."

"Okay, so Finn is going to follow up with Darby and Danny and Cait are going to talk to the people at the marina regarding Stuart. Does anyone know anyone named Ray or Bosley?" Siobhan asked.

No one by those names came to mind offhand, although Ray was a common name, and given enough time we could probably come up with a short list of local Rays.

I looked at Finn. "Did you ever find out why the sheriff is so interested in this case?"

"I'm still not sure why he seems so invested. This is the first time he's sent someone over to take the lead except for those instances when I've been off the island for one reason or another. I can't help but wonder if he's unhappy with the job I'm doing and doesn't trust me to solve this on my own. I have to admit it's causing me a fair amount of stress."

"I don't think that's it," I assured Finn. "Every murder that's taken place under your watch has been solved. We've even managed to solve some cold cases."

"Maybe we've done too good a job and the sheriff is getting suspicious," Danny suggested.

"Suspicious of what?" Siobhan asked.

"Suspicious that Finn might have help," Danny answered. "We haven't been exactly quiet about the fact that we've been conducting our own investigations. Maybe the sheriff realizes that not everything is entirely on the up and up."

"Danny might have a point," Finn added. "I've already asked Cait to keep a low profile on this case and the rest of you need to do the same thing, at least until we figure out what exactly is on the sheriff's mind."

The room fell into silence. I glanced at Tara, who looked pale. We hadn't even touched the surface tonight, but I didn't want her to overdo things, so I suggested we wrap things up and reconvene the following evening. Finn planned to follow up on a few things and Cody offered to see what he could dig up. I'd pretty much decided to close the bookstore the following day so I could focus my attention on the case. Tara was in no shape to go in and the girl we'd hired to help out over Christmas had gone to live with an aunt when her pregnancy had progressed to the point where she couldn't work, so I was the only person who could open the store. This was our slow season, though, and I felt that finding Tanner's killer took precedence over selling a few cups of coffee and a handful of books. If the person who'd run two cars off the road was a serial killer of sorts who randomly chose whoever was headed in their direction, there could be additional victims, which meant we had no time to waste.

After everyone left, Tara took Bandit and Moirai and went to bed and Cody and I decided to take the dogs out for a romp on the beach. It was a chilly night, but the sky was clear and the moon was almost full, making for a romantic evening despite the tension we were feeling.

"How was Orlando?" I asked as Cody and I walked hand in hand just above the waterline. The tide was out, so the waves rolled gently onto the shore as Max and

Rambler chased each other up and down the sandy beach.

"Hectic. Originally, I was going to stay there a few more days, but when you called last night I arranged to come home early. I might have to go back next month for a few days, but I wanted to be here with you during this difficult time."

"And I appreciate that. I know what you're doing is very important, but I hate it when you're away."

"I know." Cody stopped walking and pulled me into his arms. "I missed you too. I'd ask you to come with me, but I work really long hours when I'm there and I'm afraid you'd be bored."

"I'm sure I could keep myself entertained and I'd like to come along at some point, but with Tara being laid up, it'll be a while before I can take any time off work. I'm going to close the store tomorrow so I can focus all my efforts on figuring out who ran Tanner and Tara off the road, but we can't afford to close Coffee Cat Books for too many days."

"Now that Danny's boat has been leased maybe he can pitch in at the store, at least until Tara is back on her feet."

"That's actually a really good idea. I couldn't leave him there alone because he doesn't know how to make the coffee drinks, but he can certainly help with cleaning and stocking shelves. If I know Tara, though, she won't stay away for long. Even with her arm in a sling I'm sure she'll be down there supervising before too long."

"Are you ready to turn around? I've been up since three this morning East Coast time. I think my body is beginning to shut down."

"Yeah, okay." I called the dogs to let them know we were changing direction. "By the way, I have something to share with you if you aren't too tired. Actually, a couple of somethings."

Cody glanced at me. "I'm awake for the time being. What's on your mind?"

"First of all, I took my mom to look at a house she's interested in buying."

"That's nice." Cody yawned. "Did she like it?"

"She did. In fact, she wants to make an offer on it. And there's more. The guy who's selling the house: I think he might just turn out to be the man my mom has been looking for."

Cody stopped walking and looked at me. "The man your mom has been looking for?"

I explained about the chemistry the couple seemed to share and how I'd instinctively known Mom and Gabe were destined to be together. Maybe after a couple of years of working with Tansy's cats some of their magic had rubbed off on me and I too was gaining the ability to see the future. I could see Cody was doubtful despite what I'd thought was an excellent explanation of what I'd observed.

Cody put his arm around me and we resumed our walk. "Okay, you've convinced me. You said there were two things you wanted to tell me."

"The second thing is a much bigger deal. It has to do with a secret I've been keeping for Maggie and Father Kilian for a whole lot longer than I've cared to. What I'm about to tell you is still a secret—I guess part of it will always be a secret—so you have to promise not to tell anyone what I'm about to tell you."

"Okay."

"I guess you know Father Kilian is planning to retire."

"You've mentioned something about that before."

"What I didn't tell you then is that he's also leaving the priesthood. Not immediately, but eventually." I stopped walking and turned to face Cody, sensing his confusion. "That's so he can marry the love of his life, who, it turns out, is my Aunt Maggie."

"I've always wondered if there wasn't something between the two of them."

I was surprised to hear Cody say that because it seemed to me that Maggie and Father Kilian had done an excellent job of keeping their feelings to themselves, but Cody was very observant, and if there was something to notice he'd be the one to do it. I filled him in on the rest of the story as we walked back toward Mr. Parsons's house and Cody's third-floor apartment. I was happy to find Cody was both supportive and understanding of what Father Kilian and Maggie planned to do over the course of the next year or so. I knew the parishioners at St. Patrick's wouldn't be as understanding, and there was a part of me that was dreading the day Father Kilian announced the final phase of his plans. As it was, his announcement that he was retiring was sure to cause an uproar the following Sunday.

Chapter 6

Tuesday, February 7

Cody got up early and went into the office so he could check in with the part-time help he'd hired to get the paper out while he was in Florida. His trips were planned well in advance, so he was able to ensure there were plenty of articles to run and the advertising was up to date before he left. All the part-time employees had to do was add any last-minute news stories to the preformatted paper, then print and distribute the physical copies in a timely manner. Most of the time there wasn't any breaking news that would require a major reformation once it had been formatted, but with two serious accidents in the past two days, Cody wanted to write a front-page feature before the midweek edition was published the following day.

Tara was still in bed when I got up, so I left a note letting her know I'd make breakfast as soon as I returned from taking Max and Rambler for a short run.

She'd been awake when Cody and I had returned from our walk the night before, so I'd told her about my plans to close the store on Tuesday, which she seemed to be fine with. Tara wasn't one to close the store on any unscheduled days, but the accident seemed to have drained her of both her energy and her enthusiasm. I was really worried about the way the accident and Tanner's death had affected her emotionally.

I tossed a large stick into the waves for the dogs to retrieve, then paused to look out toward the morning sea. There were dark clouds on the horizon and I'd heard there was a storm expected. I was fairly sure I'd closed all the windows and secured the deck furniture before leaving my cabin the previous day, but I wasn't 100 percent certain, and with a storm headed our way I realized I'd better stop there on my way into town.

I'd contemplated asking Francine Rivers to come over to sit with Tara again. I hated to leave her alone while Danny and I visited the marina, but Sister Mary had called and offered to spend the day with Tara, leaving me free to follow any leads I was able to dig up.

I called to the dogs and headed back toward Mr. Parsons's house. He'd been moving around in his bedroom when I'd stopped to pick up Rambler, so I decided to check on him before going back upstairs to Cody's apartment. Mr. Parsons's home was huge, and Cody had remodeled the third floor, turning it into a very nice apartment that had access both from the inside and via a stairway down the exterior of the house. It was a perfect situation. Cody and Mr. Parsons were as close as any grandfather and grandson and the apartment allowed Cody to keep an eye on the elderly man while still maintaining a degree of privacy.

"Mr. Parsons," I called as I entered the house.

"In the kitchen."

I headed down the hallway with both dogs on my heels.

"Coffee?" Mr. Parsons offered.

"No, thanks. I need to get upstairs to check on Tara, but I wanted to see if you needed anything before I did."

"Cody left an egg casserole I just need to heat up."

Cody took such good care of Mr. Parsons, and really all the people in his life. I think that was one of the things I loved the most about him.

"There's a storm on the way, so I'll check your windows before I leave. Sister

Mary is coming to sit with Tara. I'm not sure if she'll get here before I go, and she may come to the main door, so it would be great if you could listen for her."

"Happy to. How's Tara today?"

"She was still sleeping when I took the dogs out, but I imagine she's still feeling pretty sore. The poor thing really is beat up."

"If she needs anything while you're away she can use the intercom to call down to me. I'll keep an ear out just in case."

I doubted Mr. Parsons could make the trip up the two flights of stairs, but it was sweet of him to offer. As promised, I made a quick check of Mr. Parsons's windows before I headed upstairs, just in case the storm arrived before Cody got home. It turned out everything was already locked up tight, but better safe than sorry.

"How was your run?" Tara, who was sitting on the sofa in front of the fire, asked as I walked into the apartment.

"Quick but nice. There's a storm coming. I've checked all the windows and Mr. Parsons knows about it, so there shouldn't be any problems."

"Do you need me to do anything?" Tara asked. "Can Mr. Parsons manage should the storm arrive?"

"He actually offered to watch out for you if you needed anything, although I think you have a better chance of navigating the stairs than he does. He did say he'd listen for the intercom, and you might have Sister Mary check on him while she's here. If there's really an issue and you can't get hold of me or Cody, call Francine. She can usually get here in a couple of minutes. She may stop by anyway."

"I'll listen for her."

"I'm going to grab a shower and then I'll make us breakfast."

"Cody left an egg casserole. There was a note by the coffeemaker with instructions. I already put it in the oven. It should be ready in about fifteen minutes."

With that, I headed down the hall to get ready for the day ahead.

After Tara and I shared the casserole I called Danny to arrange for him to pick me up. I knew Max would want to come with me today, which would work out because it was a chilly day and he'd be fine if I had to leave him in the car for short periods of time. The question was what to do with Moirai. I doubted he'd be all that thrilled with driving around for a good portion of the day.

"So how about it?" I asked him. "Do you want to come with Max and me or stay here with Tara and Bandit?"

Moirai jumped onto the sofa where Tara was sitting and curled up in her lap.

"Okay, I guess you've spoken." I looked at Tara. "Danny is on his way over to pick me up. Sister Mary should be here within a half hour. You have a blanket, hot tea, and two furry kitties in your lap. Do you need anything else before I go?"

"I'll be fine," Tara assured me. "Yes, I feel like I was run over by a truck, but I'm able to get around on my own and I have my cell if I should need anything I can't get for myself before Sister Mary arrives."

"Are you sure?" I asked. Tara had an odd look on her face.

"I'm sure. I'm fine, really. I guess I'm just a little nervous about spending time with Sister Mary."

I sat down next to Tara. "You've known her most of your life. The two of you have always gotten along fantastically. I know things are a little weird now, but remember you're still you and she's still her. Nothing has to change if you don't want it to."

Tara smiled weakly. "I know, you're right. I'm sure everything will be fine once she gets here. Now, you go off with

Danny, and between the two of you figure out who killed Tanner. He might have been lying to me about the drinking and the restaurant, but he had a good heart and I really cared about him."

"Okay. If you're sure you're okay I'll head down. Call me if you need anything at all."

Danny was just pulling into the drive when I exited the house via the back steps. "I have news," he said the minute I slid into the passenger seat of his truck.

"I'm listening."

"After I left Cody's place last night I headed over to Shots to see if I could find out anything about Colton that you weren't able to. It turns out he isn't in rehab voluntarily. He told everyone he decided to check in for health purposes, but the bartender told me that he's really there as part of a plea deal to stay out of jail after receiving his third DUI."

"I guess that explains why he isn't really interested in selling the bar."

"It seems to me that Colton didn't want it getting out that he had another DUI, so he created an elaborate story about wanting to get his life together. The guy I spoke to seems to think he'll be back to his old ways the minute he gets out of rehab."

I shook my head. "I don't understand why people are so self-destructive."

"Alcoholism is a complicated disease. Some alcoholics manage to conquer it, but I'm afraid most of the ones I know live a life of peaks and valleys that mirror their tendency to get on and off the wagon."

"Tanner managed to hide the fact that he was drinking again fairly well. It never even occurred to me that he wasn't in recovery. He talked about going to meetings all the time. Tara was sure of that as well. I wonder what he was doing all those times he told us he was off to attend AA meetings."

"Probably drinking. When we get to the marina let me do the talking. As a commercial boat owner, I'm more likely to get the information we need. In fact, it might be a good idea if you waited in the car with Max."

Max barked at the sound of his name.

"I'm not waiting in the car, but I'll let you do the talking."

Danny pulled into the mostly empty parking lot. During the summer you couldn't get a spot, but during the winter the marina operated at a minimal capacity.

"Stuart around?" Danny asked the employee who was manning the office.

"Stuart doesn't work here anymore. Can I help you with something?"

Danny leaned his elbows on the counter before answering. "I run Hart of the Sea Tours out of Pelican Bay Marina."

"I know who you are."

"I leased my boat for a few months, but it looks like I might have a gig at the end of the month and I was hoping Stuart would give me a deal on a short-term rental."

"How big a rig are you talking?"

"Fifteen, maybe twenty passengers."

"I know someone who might be willing to rent you something that would work. I'll have to check with the owner, but if you want to leave your number I'll call you back."

Danny grabbed a pen off the counter and jotted down his cell phone number on the back of a business card. "Thanks; I appreciate it. I won't know for sure if the gig is a go for another week or so, but it would be good to know what sort of rentals are out there before I commit." Danny passed the card across the counter. "I hadn't heard Stuart had quit. When did that happen?"

"He didn't quit; he got canned back in the fall. He was a good kid, but he came to work drunk one time too many, so the boss fired him. The last thing you want to have at a working marina is a drunk employee."

"I hear yah." Danny stood up straight and turned toward me.

"I'll give you a call after I hear about the boat," the man promised.

"Appreciate it."

Danny opened the door and gestured for me to go out in front of him.

"Is that it?" I asked.

"It'd seem suspicious if we started asking too many questions. He didn't bring it up, so if this Stuart is the one who had the accident he hasn't heard about it yet. And if it is, he will, and when he does, he'll remember a couple of people coming around and asking a bunch of questions. Finn said to keep a low profile."

I hurried to keep up with Danny, who had longer legs than I did. "Yeah, I guess you're right. So what now?"

Danny opened the passenger door of the truck and I slid in. "I'm not sure. I wonder if Finn has confirmed whether the Stuart who was run off the road yesterday is the one on Tanner's list."

"I can call him on his personal cell."

"It might be better to call Siobhan to find out what she knows. If the deputy the sheriff sent over is here to keep an eye on the way Finn does things, we really do need to stay off the radar."

I called Siobhan while Danny drove us back toward the peninsula. Finn hadn't been able to find out who'd bought the burner phone, and although he'd been calling the number on Tanner's list on a regular basis no one had answered yet. Siobhan indicated Finn was working on the assumption that the Stuart on the list and the one in the accident were one and the same, but so far he had no proof. He had remembered, though, that the reason the name Bosley sounded so familiar was because he'd arrested someone named Jeff Bosley for public intoxication last summer.

"Did she say whether Finn followed up with the guy from his bowling league?" Danny asked.

"She didn't mention it. Let's head over to the paper to see if Cody has managed to dig anything up," I suggested. "He said he was going to do a computer search with the information he had."

Danny turned onto the highway and headed back toward Pelican Bay. Living on a small island, it wasn't too long a drive to get from any one point to another, which was a good thing, considering the way our day was unfolding.

"You know, the common variable that seems to be emerging among the men on Tanner's list—assuming the people we've identified are the correct ones— is alcohol," Danny mused. "We know Tanner was off the wagon, Colton is in court-mandated rehab for a DUI, the Stuart who worked at the marina was fired for showing up to work drunk, and Jeff Bosley was arrested for public intoxication."

"So maybe the men on the list are just drinking buddies?"

"That would make sense."

Danny turned off the highway onto the main street running through the center of Pelican Bay. He slowed the truck a bit before resuming our conversation in a totally different place from where we'd left it off. "Aiden called me last night all up in arms about some house Mom wants to buy and the man who's selling it."

"It's a great house and Gabe is a great guy," I said. "Even Siobhan agrees. Aiden is just being Aiden; don't let him persuade you there's a problem until you check things out for yourself."

"I intend to do that. Mom has an appointment to go back for a second look today after Cassie gets out of school and I volunteered to drive them."

"Like I said, keep an open mind."

"Don't I always?"

I nodded. Danny usually did keep an open mind. In fact, of the five Hart siblings, he probably was the most open-minded and easygoing.

Danny pulled up in front of the newspaper, which was right next door to Finn's office. I noticed there were two sheriff's vehicles parked out front. It appeared the deputy the sheriff had sent was still on the island. I'd hoped he'd come over, take a look at the situation, and return home, but it looked as if we weren't going to be that lucky.

"Just the people I wanted to see," Cody greeted us as we walked in the front door.

"Do you have news?" Danny asked as I detoured around the counter to give Cody a quick kiss.

"Actually, I do. Let's lock up and head into the back. These walls are thin and I don't want anyone overhearing what I'm about to tell you."

Cody locked the door, then led us down the hallway to his office, which was located in the center of the building and so had no shared walls with the other tenants.

"What's up?" I asked when we were all seated.

"Finn stopped by shortly after I arrived this morning. He said he'd managed to track down Darby Prater, who verified that he knew Tanner and admitted they attended the same Alcoholics Anonymous meetings."

"Wait," I interrupted. "I thought Tanner was off the wagon and drinking like a fish."

"It appears he had been drinking, but Darby told Finn that people sometimes continue to attend their regular AA meetings and pretend to be sober even when they aren't."

"Why would anyone do that?"

"Some attend because they're mandated by the courts to do so, while others are lying to their families and friends about their drinking and need to keep up a front. Darby said there are even some AA members who are lying to themselves."

"I don't understand."

"They don't look at their drinking as being off the wagon but more as a stumble on the road to recovery."

"And Darby?"

"He told Finn he started going to AA meetings eight months ago, when his wife threatened to leave him, and hasn't taken a drink since."

"And the others?"

"Darby wouldn't say. There's an anonymity piece to the program that most members take seriously. Finn did think to check the sentence Jeff Bosley received when he was arrested, and a year of court-mandated AA meetings was part of it."

"Okay, so maybe all the men on Tanner's list attended meetings together," I said, "If that's the case maybe the driver who ran Tanner and Stuart off the road is an AA member also."

"Finn thinks that's a possibility," Cody said. "If the guy attends meetings hopefully someone will recognize the description of the car and we'll have our killer."

Danny frowned. "I hope it's as simple as that, but the whole thing feels anticlimactic."

I had to agree. Still, it would be nice to get the wacko who'd been running unsuspecting motorists off the road sooner rather than later.

"It seems we've identified everyone other than Ray," I commented. "I don't suppose Finn knows who he is?"

"He didn't when I spoke to him, but I think he hoped to have this case put to bed by the end of the day. He wants us to lay low and leave things to him at this point. He still isn't sure why the deputy was sent to oversee the case, but he has a bad feeling about things."

"Do you think Finn was right when he said he was afraid the sheriff had lost confidence in him?" The idea worried me. Siobhan had finally moved home and settled in after living in Seattle for years. She was engaged to Finn, who seemed to have a secure job on the island. I knew they'd been looking at homes to move into after they married and planned to start a family fairly soon. If Finn lost his job everything would change. They would most likely move off the island. Sure, Siobhan would still be the mayor, but Finn wasn't the sort to sit around and let his wife support the family.

"I doubt that's the case," Cody answered. "Finn has done an excellent job as resident deputy. I don't know why the sheriff is so interested in this case, but I'd be willing to bet it isn't a lack of confidence in Finn."

"Cody's right," Danny said. "The best way to help Finn is to take a backseat and let him put this case to bed."

"Yeah," I acknowledged. "I guess you're right."

"I know I am, which means I suddenly have a free day. I think I'll go to Maggie's and unpack before I pick up Mom and Cassie. I can drop you off on the way."

I glanced at Cody.

"I'll give Cait a ride home," Cody offered.

"Okay, then. I'll see you both later." Danny headed toward the front of the building.

"Did you get your story written?" I asked Cody.

"Yes. Finn didn't want me to include any information I may have gained from him during our conversations. It would be suspicious if I had information not available to me in my role as a newspaper reporter. The article ended up being shorter than I planned, but I understand why he doesn't want the sheriff to suspect he'd been talking to me about the case, so I did as he requested."

"It looks like we both have some unexpected free time. Any idea how we should spend it?"

Cody pulled me into his arms. "I have a few."

I leaned into Cody's embrace, then pulled slightly away when my phone buzzed, indicating I had a text. "Hold that thought," I said. The text was from Tara, letting me know she had looked all over Cody's apartment but couldn't find Moirai. She'd even checked with Mr. Parsons, but the cat seemed to have disappeared. I texted her back to tell her not to worry; Tansy's cats seemed to have their own way of doing things and I was sure he'd reappear eventually. I told her I was at the newspaper and would be home soon, and she asked if I could stop at Coffee Cat Books to pick up a few things from the office that she wanted to work on while she was laid up.

"Bad news?" Cody asked.

"Not so much bad as inconvenient news. Tara wants me to pick up some stuff at Coffee Cat Books before we head home."

"I have another hour or so of work to finish up here. Why don't you take my truck and get what you need? By the time you get back I should be ready to go. You can just leave Max with me."

I glanced at Max, who was sound asleep in the corner of Cody's office, before I stood on tiptoe to kiss Cody on the lips. "Rain check on the other?"

"Count on it."

Chapter 7

The drive from the newspaper to Coffee Cat Books was a short one. Most of the shops along Main Street had brought in their sidewalk displays when the wind picked up, announcing the impending storm. I glanced out over the marina as I pulled into one of the parking spaces in front of the bookstore. There were dark, heavy-looking clouds on the horizon. I felt a tingle up my spine as my intuition whispered that this was going to be a bad one.

The first thing I noticed after climbing down from Cody's truck was the large white cat sitting on the bench near the front door of the bookstore.

"I thought I might run into you here," I said to Moirai. "You should have let Tara know what you were doing. You scared the poor thing half to death."

"Meow." Moirai jumped off the bench and began to purr as he rubbed against my legs.

"I take it there's a reason for your visit?"

He turned and began to walk down the wharf toward Main Street.

"Wait," I shouted. "I need to get a few things for Tara and then I'll follow you."

Moirai ignored my plea and continued to trot down the wharf and around the corner.

"Dang cat," I muttered under my breath as I took off at a jog. Hopefully I would catch up with him before he disappeared from sight.

I increased my pace when I realized Moirai was more than a block ahead of me. By the time I caught up with him, I was beginning to breathe hard after the effort required to run against the strong wind. The cat turned onto Second Street and then darted into the small passageway between the buildings that emptied onto the alley that ran behind the buildings on Main. He made his way over to a battered blue wooden door and sat down in front of it.

"This is the back door to the old T-shirt shop. They went out of business almost a year ago. The shop is empty."

"Meow."

I glanced at the parking area across the street. There did seem to be a lot of cars parked near the deserted shop. I tried the handle on the door and it gave way. Moirai trotted inside and I followed, walking as quietly as I could.

The rear of the building had been used for storage and was currently empty. It was separated from the main part of the store, which had been the retail space, by a wall with a connecting door. The storage area might be empty, but I could hear voices coming from the front of the building. I slowly made my way to the door separating the two spaces and glanced inside. There were maybe twelve folding chairs arranged in a circle, each occupied by an adult male. Half of the group had their backs to me and I didn't recognize any of the men facing me with the exception of Ray Green, a parishioner at St. Patrick's. I stood perfectly still so as not to be detected as I listened to the conversation. It took me only a few minutes to understand what was going on: I was observing an AA meeting. If he was the Ray from Tanner's list this could very well be the group he'd attended.

"I guess you all heard about Tanner," a man wearing a dark blue beanie and a dark hooded sweatshirt said.

The others mumbled in agreement.

"I can't reveal my source," the man added, "but I have it on good authority that Tanner had been drinking when the accident occurred."

The general mumbling continued.

"I don't think Tanner had quite as good a grip on his alcoholism as he led us to believe," another man, whose back was to me, added.

"If you ask me, Tanner was an accident waiting to happen," the first man agreed. "He admitted to us that he'd fallen back into old habits."

"I told you we shouldn't allow him to continue to come to the group," a man with a yellow shirt closest to me but with his back to me commented. "It just wasn't right for him to come in every week and confess that he'd fallen off the wagon only to come back the next week and do the exact same thing."

"The meeting is open to all who are called to attend and Tanner's struggle with his journey toward sobriety was a personal one that we shouldn't be discussing in his absence," a man with a red plaid shirt reminded everyone. "Some of us will conquer our demons; others will perish in the effort. Who would like to share?"

The guy in plaid seemed to be a leader of sorts. I felt like a voyeur, watching what was meant to be a personal and anonymous discourse, so I decided to sneak out the way I'd come in. I looked around for Moirai, who had disappeared. He didn't seem to have wandered into the meeting, so I hoped I'd find him back in the alley.

When I left the building I saw Moirai sitting near a black, two-door, midsized car. It could have been the one I'd seen run Tanner off the road, but there were a lot of dark-colored, midsized cars on the island. It couldn't hurt to take down the license plate number, so I took out my phone and snapped a photo of it. Then I looked in the windows in case something stood out, jarring a memory.

A pack of cigarettes rested on the dashboard and a half-empty bottle of water waited in the cup holder. There was a dark-colored jacket on the backseat next to a metal file box. The car's doors were locked, so there was no way to know what was inside the box, but it seemed odd that anyone would be driving around with a bunch of files, especially in this day and age, when most files were digitized.

"Can I help you with something?" a man dressed in black asked. I'd noticed him in the meeting, but he hadn't spoken.

I let out a little screech as I jumped before turning around. I placed my hand over my chest before I answered. "No. I thought this was a friend's car, but once I looked inside I realized it wasn't."

"I saw you inside, poking your head in through the door. You know that the second A in AA stands for anonymous?"

"I know. I'm sorry. I didn't mean to pry. My cat ran in through the back door, which had been left open, and when I went in to get him I heard people talking. As soon as I realized why the group had met I left."

The man looked at me with an expression that clearly communicated that he didn't believe a word I'd said. I didn't recognize him, but he did seem familiar. Madrona Island had a small population and over time we're all likely to run into everyone else. Perhaps the man worked at a business I patronized, or maybe he'd shopped in the bookstore.

"I should be going," I volunteered as he stood perfectly still, staring at me as if he were trying to figure out where he knew me from as well.

I turned and walked away.

Just as I was rounding the corner, he climbed into his car and started the engine. The last thing I heard as he peeled away was country music blaring from the partially open window.

As soon as I arrived at Coffee Cat Books, I called Finn to give him the license plate number I'd pulled. He once again advised me to keep a low profile and I reminded him that the cats that seemed to come my way mostly had minds of their own. He assured me he'd run the plate, then let me know that from this point forward I should share information with him through Siobhan. He also warned me that the deputy the sheriff had sent over planned to contact me regarding an interview, probably before the end of the day. Instinctively, I didn't trust him and wasn't looking forward to speaking to him, but I didn't suppose I had a lot of choice in the matter and, in some ways, preferred to just get it over with.

I grabbed the files and paperwork Tara wanted from the bookstore office, then loaded the cat in the truck. I jumped as a clap of thunder rumbled through the sky.

I'd lived on the island all my life and had been witness to many storms, but there was something about the energy of this one I found alarming. I was about to climb into the driver's seat of Cody's truck when the man who owned the deli down the street pulled up beside me.

"Looks like we're in for quite a ride."

I glanced at the dark clouds gathering overhead. "Yeah. I was just thinking the same thing."

"Guy on the television said we should expect hurricane force winds and up to fifteen inches of rain. I imagine we'll have some flooding before this is over."

"It sounds like it." I decided in that moment to check on Aunt Maggie and Francine. The road connecting the peninsula to the rest of the island often flooded during heavy rain. It would be prudent to make certain they both had all the supplies they might need should the peninsula become isolated for a day or more.

"I noticed you were closed today."

"I'm not sure if you heard, but Tara was in an auto accident. We were closed today, but I plan to open tomorrow."

"Honestly, I wouldn't bother. I've pretty much decided to close the deli tomorrow. I doubt I'll have much business, and why even hassle with trying to drive in the storm?"

"You have a point."

"I talked to a couple of the other merchants in the area and they were thinking the same thing. There's talk the ferry service will be suspended during the storm. If folks can't come to the island, businesses that serve the ferry won't generate much income anyway."

"Another good point." I glanced once again into the sky. If this were a movie there would be ominous music playing in the background right about now. "Thanks for the heads-up. I think as long as I'm here I'll go ahead and post a notice that we'll remain closed until after the storm."

"Good idea. Stay safe."

"Yeah. You too."

I slid into the driver's seat of the truck and pulled up the weather app on my phone to verify what I'd been told before placing the note on the front door. Sure enough, the National Weather Service was calling for a significant weather event over the next thirty-six to forty-eight hours, with major flooding in low-lying areas.

"I'm going to run back in and put a note on the door about the closure," I said to Moirai. "I'll just be a minute."

I hurried inside, drafted the note, and placed it on the front door. Then I called Maggie, who had heard the weather report herself and planned to close the Bait and Stitch as well. Marley planned to stay with her and she'd invited Francine to bring her cats and stay with her as well should there be a blackout. Danny was staying with Maggie because he'd had to move out of his boat, which made me feel a lot better about the whole thing. I called my mother to see if she needed anything before the storm hit, although her condo was in the center of town and therefore not subject to the flooding or wind events that might affect those of us right on the water.

Once I made sure everyone I cared the most about was prepared to weather the storm, I returned to the truck and headed back toward the newspaper to pick up Cody and Max. As I drove, the first of what would turn out to be many raindrops began to fall. I turned to look at the cat. "No use both of us getting wet. Why don't you wait here? I should only be a minute."

"Meow."

"Yes, I have a bad feeling about things too." I watched as the rain began to fall harder. I'd hoped we'd have this mystery wrapped up before the storm settled over the island. "I feel like we've been communicating okay, but I do wish you could speak English, or maybe I could learn to speak cat. It would simplify things quite a bit."

The cat curled up on the passenger seat and began to purr. I'd reached over to give him a scratch behind the ears when I saw Finn motioning me to come inside from the other side of the front window of his office.

"It looks like the hour of reckoning is here. Wish me luck."

I pulled my jacket around myself, opened the truck door, and then dashed into Finn's office for what I assumed would be the previously mentioned interview.

"Caitlin Hart, this is Deputy Strong." Finn introduced the man in the deputy's uniform as I ran in through the front door. "He'd like to speak to you about the accident you witnessed the evening of February fifth."

It seemed so odd to have Finn being so formal, but I guessed a more professional tone was to be expected.

"I'm happy to speak to you, but I need to call my boyfriend first." I glanced at the short man, who ran his hand through his thinning blond hair. "He's waiting for me next door."

"You can go ahead with the interview and I'll let Cody know what's going on," Finn offered.

"You won't be joining us?"

"No. Deputy Strong will handle things."

"Okay. Tell Cody Moirai is in the truck. He may as well bring him in."

Finn offered me a look of sympathy as I followed Deputy Strong into Finn's office.

The deputy motioned for me to take a seat on the opposite side of the desk from the chair he took. He started off by asking me the same questions Finn had about my name, age, and connection with the victim in the taped interview. His monotonous voice and expressionless face did little to tell me what he was thinking. I had a feeling this was going to be a long interview.

Deputy Strong next asked me who had been present at the dinner prior to the accident and when each person left. As Finn had, he asked me to tell him what I had seen the night of the accident once we left my mother's house. He wanted a description of the car and the individual who had been driving it. I found myself beginning to relax as the interview continued to review the information I'd already provided. Maybe the whole thing would be nothing more than a repetition of the things I had already shared.

"Had you been drinking on the night of the accident?" Deputy Strong asked.

I hesitated before answering. "Drinking?"

"Had you consumed alcohol on the night of the accident?" he clarified.

"I had a glass of wine with dinner, but I certainly wasn't drunk, if that's what you're asking."

He frowned and jotted down some notes. "Do you often drink and drive?"

"I don't drink and drive. Not ever. At least not in the way you're inferring. I had one glass of wine with dinner an hour before I drove home. That in no way impaired my ability to drive."

He didn't respond, but he did write down some more notes.

"Is this relevant to the discussion at hand?" I finally asked.

"I'm simply ascertaining your value as a witness to what occurred."

"I can assure you that I saw what I saw. I wasn't drunk. I wasn't buzzed. I wasn't anything."

He raised one eyebrow and continued to make notes.

"Are you going to put the fact that I was drinking and driving in the report? Because if you do, it could hinder my ability to act as a witness once we catch this guy."

"Perhaps you should have thought of that before you got behind the wheel of a car after consuming alcohol."

"I told you I was perfectly fine to drive. Am I in some sort of trouble for this?"

"No." Deputy Strong pursed his lips. "Deputy Finnegan neglected to conduct a blood alcohol test on the night of the accident, so there isn't anything that can be done at this point. I would, however, like to remind you that any amount of alcohol in your system can impair judgment."

I didn't argue because I didn't know if that was technically true or not. It seemed like the guy was intentionally trying to shake me and was using the wine as a way to do it. I took a deep breath, sat back, and waited for the next question. Caitlin Hart didn't rattle easily and this guy was about to find that out.

"The victim, Mr. Woodson, was legally intoxicated at the time of the accident. Were you aware of that?"

"Not at the time."

"Is it possible the car heading north simply pulled onto the road and Mr. Woodson, in his intoxicated state, misjudged the situation and ended up in the ravine?"

"It's possible."

"Do you think that's what occurred?"

"No."

"You stated that the car headed straight toward Mr. Woodson in a deliberate attempt to run him off the road."

"Yes."

"Have you considered driver error rather than criminal intent as the cause of the accident?"

"Driver error?"

"Is it possible the driver of the oncoming vehicle unintentionally veered into Mr. Woodson's lane?"

"I suppose it's possible, but I don't think that's what happened."

"Would you be able to pick the driver out of a lineup?"

"No. I didn't see the driver."

"Would you be able to pick the car out of a lineup of vehicles of a similar model and color?"

"No. I didn't get a good look at the car."

"Is there anything about that night you do remember with clarity?"

Again, I had the feeling he was insinuating I didn't have a clear mind on the night of the accident. "No."

He sat and stared at me, as if daring me not to flinch. I sat perfectly still as I waited for him to make his next move. I wasn't sure what he hoped to accomplish by treating me as a suspect rather than a witness, but maybe he had no personality and treated everyone with the same cool detachment.

"Okay," Deputy Strong said at last. "You're free to go. I'll be in touch."

I got up and walked out the door, suppressing the urge to cry until I had made it safely to the newspaper next door.

Chapter 8

Later that evening Cody, Danny, Tara, and I were sitting around Cody's dining table listening to the rain slam into the window as Danny told us his experience with Gabe Williams earlier in the day. Not only did Danny approve of the man and the house but my talkative brother had come away with quite a bit of information about Gabe as well.

"He has three children. His oldest son is involved in international finance and lives in Singapore, the other son is a commercial pilot stationed out of Los Angeles, and his daughter is a general practitioner in Portland."

"Did they grow up here?" Tara asked.

"No. Gabe and his wife moved to Madrona Island after all the children had left home. They bought the house Gabe is selling and fixed it up. He said himself it was a labor of love as well as a means of moving on to the next stage of their life, after all the children had flown the nest."

"And then his wife died," I provided.

"She passed away a year and a half ago, after a brief battle with cancer."

"And Gabe has lived in the house alone this whole time?" Tara wondered.

"No. He's spent very little time in the house until recently. He traveled and spent time with each of his children after his wife passed and returned to the island just prior to the holidays. It was at that point that his daughter began to put pressure on him to sell the house and move closer to where she lives. I could tell he was having second thoughts."

"And Cassie?" I asked. "What did she think about the house?"

Danny shrugged. "She isn't as enamored of Gabe as you and Siobhan seem to be, but she seemed to like him, and she said the house was really great and one of her favorite beaches to hang out at is basically across the street. I think if Mom pursues either the house or the man she'll probably warm up to the idea."

"So now we just need to work on grumpy Aiden," I said.

"I don't think we need to do anything. It's Mom's potential house, Mom's potential man, and Mom's life. I think we should let her take the lead on this."

I hated it when Danny was right at the cost of me being wrong. I was about to suggest paving the way when a clap of thunder was followed by a rumbling echo and flickering lights.

"That one sounded close," I observed. I looked at Cody. "Do you think Mr. Parsons is okay?"

"I'm sure he's fine. Banjo and Summer are with him. Their place is in a low spot that tends to flood during heavy rain, so they're going to stay here for a few days. They planned to watch old movies."

Francine and Marley were with Maggie, so I thought I could stop worrying about everyone and get back to our conversation.

"Were you able to speak to Finn after your interview?" Danny asked me a few minutes later.

"No. The opportunity didn't present itself. I did call Siobhan, and she said she'd try to get an update and call me later. This whole thing really has me on edge."

"It does seem there's more going on than appears on the surface," Cody agreed. "I wonder if Finn managed to find out who the car you saw at the AA meeting belonged to."

"I wouldn't think it would be difficult to find out. If I had to guess..." I paused as my phone rang. "It's Siobhan," I informed the others and then answered the call, putting it on speakerphone. "Any news?"

"Some. Finn is pretty upset about what's going on with the investigation and really doesn't want any of us involved, but he was called out to respond to a 911 call, so I thought I'd take advantage of his absence to call you. The plates on the car you found belong to a guy named Harvey Pruitt. He's new to the island, so I don't have a ton of information on him. It looks like he moved here from Walla Walla four months ago. Finn spoke to him, but he insisted he doesn't know anything about either accident. You admitted you didn't see anything specific and there are a lot of dark-colored cars on the island, so there isn't much Finn can do."

"Does Pruitt have an alibi?"

"He said he was home."

"Has the other guy, Stuart, regained consciousness?"

"I'm afraid he died this morning. Finn did show a photo of him to Darby, who said he'd never seen him before, so Finn is thinking at this point that he isn't in the same AA group as the others and may not be the Stuart on Tanner's list."

I let out a long breath. If the Stuart on the list wasn't the one who'd died maybe the list had nothing to do with the two accidents at all.

"I'm afraid the man I spoke to outside the AA meeting may not be the person we're looking for," I said after I hung up with Siobhan. "It doesn't appear the Stuart from the accident attended the same AA meeting as the other individuals we've identified from Tanner's list."

Danny shrugged. "I guess Tanner's list might not have anything to do with the accidents."

"What now?" Tara asked.

"I'm not sure." I curled my legs up under my body as I settled onto the sofa. Just a few hours earlier it had seemed this mystery was about to be solved and now I felt like we were back to square one. I still believed the answer lay with finding the link between Tanner and Stuart Evans, though, so I asked Cody to log on to his computer to see what he could find out about the second victim.

Cody began pulling up various documents associated with the name. It took him several minutes before he started to speak. "As we know, Evans moved to the island last spring after obtaining a job at Harthaven Marina. According to the man Danny spoke to, he was laid off after showing up drunk one too many times, although his unemployment form indicates he was laid off due to a reduction in the workload at the marina. It looks like he was still on unemployment, so I'm going to assume he never got another job. There's a lease at the Bayside Apartments under his name that runs out next month."

"Is that it?" I asked.

"So far."

"It's not a lot." I looked at Danny. "Maybe someone else who works at the marina established a personal relationship with him."

"I can ask around."

"I may be chasing windmills, but it seems to me it would be helpful to know about his hobbies and interests. Did he belong to a bowling league, attend a book club, own a motorcycle? His link to Tanner could very well be buried somewhere among all the seemingly unimportant details about his life."

"A lot of the guys from both marinas end up at O'Malley's at the end of the day. I'll head over there to see what I can find out. In fact, if we're done I'll go now. I could use a little of the hard stuff and all Cody seems to have is beer and wine."

"I don't think you should be drinking hard stuff and then driving home in this storm," I scolded the younger of my brothers.

Danny winked. "I'm sure I can find a place to stay."

Yeah, I bet he could. Danny had women stashed in every corner of Madrona Island and, surprisingly, none of them seemed to mind that he liked to play the field.

After Danny left, Cody, Tara, and I tossed around some theories. None seemed to stand out over any of the others, which didn't give us a firm direction for the next day. Of course, with the way the storm was coming together, I doubted any of us would be driving anywhere, let alone investigating the accidents because we were supposed to be laying low.

"Maybe we should talk to Stuart's neighbors at the Bayside Apartments," Cody suggested. "If he lived there the entire time he'd been on the island chances are he met people and developed friendships."

"Weather permitting, we can do that tomorrow," I agreed.

"And maybe we should check out Tanner's place again," Tara added.

"We could do that, although Moirai seemed content with the items I found. I doubt there's anything more to find."

"So the only thing you found there was the list?"

"And the tackle box."

"Tackle box?"

"Honestly, I sort of forgot about it. It's just a tackle box. It's back at my place. I can get it tomorrow if we want to take another look at it."

"There must be a reason the cat pointed it out," Tara insisted.

"True. Although…" I looked down at my phone, which had started to buzz. "It's Siobhan again," I said. "Hey, what's up?" I asked, again setting it on speakerphone.

"I just spoke to Finn. It turns out the 911 call he responded to was another auto accident."

"Same MO?"

"Finn didn't know. There were no witnesses, and the victim—a woman this time—was out cold. A passing motorist noticed headlights coming from the bottom of the ravine and called 911."

"The same ravine Tanner and Tara ended up in?"

"The exact same one. It's pouring and visibility is close to nil, so the woman could very well have misjudged the road.

Still, the fact that the accident occurred in almost the exact same spot seems suspect."

"Very suspect."

"Finn's heading over to the hospital to see what he can find out about the victim. He said she didn't appear to have any serious injuries, so he's hoping she'll regain consciousness and tell him what happened. The main reason he called was to let me know he'll be late. I'm not sure I'll be able to get back to you again tonight, but if I can't, I'll call you in the morning."

"Okay. Great. And thanks for keeping us in the loop. I know this thing with the off-island deputy must be difficult."

"It is."

Tara went to bed after I got off the phone, and Cody and I decided to brave the storm to take the dogs out for one final bathroom break before settling in for the night. The wind was still blowing in from offshore, but the rain had temporarily slowed to a drizzle. I pulled my raincoat on over my sweatshirt and jeans and tucked my long hair up under the hood. I was under no illusion that this walk was going to be a pleasant one, but the dogs needed to go out regardless of the weather.

The moonless sky was inky dark, illuminated occasionally by a flash of horizontal lightning that reflected off the clouds but didn't appear below. I could hear the rumble of thunder as we encouraged the dogs to be quick in their venture.

"It always makes me nervous when the lightning stays up in the clouds like that. I feel much better when I can actually see where it is," I shouted against the noise created by the wind.

"It does make for a spooky feeling," Cody agreed. "I remember a particularly eerie time when I was crossing an open desert with the SEALs. Six of us were dispatched to rescue two members of our squad who had been captured during night maneuvers. It had been a hot day and it was still a warm night despite the storm, which had blown in just after we reached the halfway point. I remember how exposed we felt when we realized there was lightning all around us, with no shelter in sight. We figured we'd be safest inside the vehicles, but staying put when you don't know if the next lightning strike is going to be the one that hits you isn't easy to do."

"It sounds horrible. Where were you?"

Cody squeezed my hand. "It's classified, but trust me when I tell you that particular desert isn't somewhere I'm eager to return. As it turned out, the lightning was the least of our worries that night, but I'm afraid that's classified as well."

"Are you making this whole thing up?"

"Absolutely not. Why would you say that?"

"Telling me something is classified just seems so covert. I guess I never stopped to think about what it was you were doing all that time you were in the Navy. I'm sort of glad I didn't know the kinds of things you were doing. I'm sure I would have been worried."

"I thought you hated me while I was away."

"I didn't hate you. I wanted to, but deep down I would have been worried if I had stopped to think for one minute what it meant to be a SEAL."

"I won't try to tell you I wasn't in any real danger because I was. But I will say it's the memory of that danger the makes me so determined to incorporate some of my ideas into the training program. A lot of the things I learned early on helped me to survive later in my career when things were particularly tense. I hope to use some of the techniques and strategies I learned through trial and error to better prepare the men and women who have been recruited before they even embark on their first mission."

"You're a good guy, Cody West." I leaned over and kissed him. "Do you think the dogs have had enough time? The rain is starting to pick up again and I'd prefer not to get any wetter than I already am."

"Yeah, I think we have—" Cody's reply was cut off by a flash of lightning and a loud clap of thunder. "That was close."

"Too close. It looked like it hit over at Maggie's." I took off down the beach at a run. It didn't take Cody and the dogs long to catch up with me. "What if it hit the house?" I yelled as I continued to run.

"I have longer legs than you, so I can get there faster. Meet me there."

Cody pulled ahead of me with Rambler following, but Max stayed with me. I was running as fast as I could, which was pretty fast, but Cody was faster. When I arrived at Maggie's house I could see that the lightning had hit a Madrona tree, and one of its limbs had fallen onto the Harthaven Cat Sanctuary. Maggie was standing next to Cody, assessing the damage.

"We should get inside," Cody said to both Maggie and me.

"The cats," Maggie cried.

"The structure looks sound, although there could be a small leak in the roof where the branch hit," Cody shouted above the wind.

"I'll check on them," I said before jogging to the front door of the sanctuary. When I entered everything looked okay, although the cats were pacing and crying. The noise had definitely disturbed them. I went into the community recreation area, where all the cats, except those with kittens and the meanest feral cats, who could not be trusted with the others, were allowed to mingle. They all ran to me and I dropped to the floor, offering comfort to as many as I could. Cody and Maggie entered the building right behind me. We were all soaked to the skin, but making sure the cats were all right seemed the most important thing at that moment.

"I need to check on Stella," Maggie said. "She's a new addition who seemed to be in the early stages of labor when I checked on the cats earlier. I moved her to the nursery."

"I'm going to take the dogs over to your cabin, then come back to take a closer look at the roof where the limb hit," Cody informed me.

"Okay. I'll wait here and do what I can to help Maggie."

Cody settled both dogs into my cabin and returned to the cat sanctuary, where he located a small leak. He found some heavy tarps to temporarily patch the roof, while I continued to speak softly to the cats. The sound of thunder was now farther to our north. It seemed the strong cell that had passed overhead had moved on by this point. It continued to rain, but the wind had lessened considerably.

"Cait, I need your help," Maggie said a short time later.

I got up from the floor and followed her into the nursery. "What's wrong?"

"Stella seems to be in distress. The kittens should be coming, but so far they haven't. I need to check her, but I need you to hold her still."

I grabbed the poor cat's front feet and held her down the best I could while Maggie checked her progress. She was crying with what I assumed was fear and agony, but I knew Maggie was doing the best she could. The lights flickered and I prayed the power would hold on for at least a while longer. The cat sanctuary had a generator, but it required someone to physically start it and transfer the power source, and at this point everyone's hands were full.

"It feels like the kitten is turned. I'm going to rotate it. This is going to hurt, so hold on to Stella tight. We don't want her getting up and injuring herself."

I spoke softly to the poor animal, who wouldn't be comforted as Maggie did what she needed to do. A few seconds later a kitten poured out of the mother's body.

"Continue to hold her. She looks terrified and I don't want her getting away from us. She has a couple more."

I continued to talk softly to the cat as I held her still, and Maggie helped deliver the remainder of the kittens. Once all of them were free of the mother, Maggie told me to let her go. She immediately jumped up and ran under a nearby cabinet.

"Let's give her a minute to adjust to the situation." Maggie made sure all the kittens were breathing freely. "Let's sneak out and see what she does. We can watch through the window."

We left, and the cat continued to hide for several minutes, then ever so slowly crawled out from under the cabinet. She looked at the door suspiciously as she made her way back to the bed Maggie had prepared for the kittens. At some point she must have realized we weren't coming back because she joined her babies and set to giving them all baths while they chowed down on their first meal.

"The roof is patched and should be fine until we can make a more permanent repair," Cody said when he joined us, as Maggie and I watched the new family through the window. "The cats in the common area seem to have settled down, but Moose is pacing around quite a bit, so you might want to check on him. I would have tried to comfort him, but he hates me. The last time I tried to pet him I ended up with a deep scratch on my arm for my effort."

Moose was an old feral who was set in his ways and pretty much hated everyone. He was a permanent member of the shelter because he was too stubborn to be socialized enough to join an adopted home. He wasn't overly fond of me either, but he loved Maggie, who went to go talk him down.

"Is everyone going to be okay?" Cody asked.

"Yeah. I think the thunder, followed by the branch hitting the roof, freaked everyone out, but it seems like they're all settling back down."

"I took a peek at the weather map on my phone. It looks like the worst of the storm has passed for tonight at least. We're expecting more rain through the night, but the wind and lightning should die down until tomorrow, when the second wave of the storm is supposed to hit."

"And then?"

"And then it looks like we're in for at least another day of rain that will stagger in intensity from gale force to light sprinkles."

"It's a good thing I put a note on the door of the bookstore, letting everyone know we were going to be closed."

"If tomorrow's storm is as bad as they're predicting I doubt anyone will be out shopping anyway."

Cody and I stayed a while longer to ensure that the cats had all calmed down and Maggie, Marley, and Francine were settled as well, then we grabbed the dogs and the tackle box and headed back down the beach. Maggie had offered to drive us home, but we were already wet to the skin, so having her get out her car didn't seem worth the effort. As soon as we arrived at Mr. Parsons's house, Cody went to check on him and his guests, while I headed upstairs for a hot shower.

I was just washing the conditioner from my hair when Cody came into the bathroom.

"I'm almost done," I said aloud when I heard him moving around on the other side of the shower curtain. "I'll hurry."

"Actually," Cody said as he slid into the shower beside me, "I had something else in mind."

Chapter 9

Wednesday, February 8

I woke the next morning to the sound of a steady downpour. The wind had lessened and the electrical activity we'd had the previous night seemed to have quieted, but I had a feeling the flooding the weather center had predicted was going to be a reality rather than just a possibility. I could hear Tara and Cody chatting in the next room, so I slipped on some warm sweats and joined them.

"Coffee?" Cody asked.

"Please."

"It's really coming down out there," Tara commented, voicing the same things I'd been thinking. "I guess it's a good thing we planned to be closed today. I doubt we would have had much business anyway."

"The weather report on the news is predicting another cell this afternoon as strong as the one we had last night," Cody added.

"Are you going into town?" I asked. Wednesday was normally the day Cody printed and distributed the paper's midweek edition.

"I'm going in this morning. My plan is to have the paper printed and distributed and to be back home by the time the stronger cell hits."

"I'll go with you to help," I offered. I glanced at Tara. "As long as I can find someone to keep Tara company."

"You guys go on ahead," Tara said. "I'm feeling better today. I think I'll go downstairs and watch movies with Mr. Parsons, Banjo, and Summer. Summer mentioned they planned to watch some old Debbie Reynolds movies today. I love her."

I glanced at Cody. "Okay. Just give me a few minutes to dress and I'll be ready."

"I think we should cancel choir tonight," Cody said. "I'll start calling everyone while you're getting ready."

The drive into town was a dicey one. There were already sections of road covered with floodwater. Cody knew the route well and took it slow, making detours when necessary to avoid the areas most impacted by standing water. By the time we pulled up in front of the newspaper the rain had lessened somewhat, although a glance at the sky indicated we were experiencing only a temporary lull.

"Finn's car is here. I'm going to go chat with him before his sidekick shows up," I told Cody. "I won't be long."

"Okay. I have to do the final formatting, so there isn't anything for you to do until the newspapers are ready for bundling and delivery anyway."

Luckily, Finn was the only one in his office when I arrived. "Did Tonto go home?"

Finn looked up from the desk, where he'd been working on his computer. "He left on the last ferry yesterday. I think he was planning on coming in today, but the ferries aren't running due to the storm. It looks like I'll have a break from his oversight today."

I sat down on one of the guest chairs. "Did the woman in the accident last night regain consciousness?"

"Yes, and it looks like she's going to be okay. They're keeping her in the hospital until tomorrow for observation because she was unconscious for quite some time, but the doctor I spoke to said she should be just fine."

"That's good. Could she tell you what happened?"

Finn sat back in his chair. "She said she was driving home from her theater group when a car seemed to come out of nowhere. It was coming at her head-on, so she swerved to avoid it and ended up in the ravine. She was lucky; her car got hung up on a tree, so it didn't fall all the way to the bottom the way Tanner's did."

"Did she remember anything about the car?"

"Nope. She said she was driving along and all of a sudden there were headlights coming toward her. She couldn't remember anything else about the car."

I leaned forward and rested my elbows on the desk. "Okay, so whoever is doing this is either randomly selecting cars to run off the road or he or she has a way of knowing exactly where the victims will be and when."

Finn paused before answering. I could see he'd been giving the matter thought. "At first, when we had just two victims, I suspected the incidents were linked, but now I'm not so sure. I showed the victim, whose name is Celeste Waters, photos of both Tanner and Stuart. She claimed not to know either of them. I asked her about her daily routine, hoping to stumble onto something the three had in common, but I didn't find anything that stood out. She works as a bartender at that new pub on the north shore."

"The Port-O-Call?"

"Yeah, that's the one. Tanner and Stuart were both the sort to spend time in bars, but she says she'd never seen either of them in the one where she worked. At least not while she was on duty."

"Still, the common link seems to be alcohol."

"That occurred to me as well."

"What else do you know about her?"

Finn opened a file on top of his desk. "She's twenty-seven and single. She moved to the island a year ago after a bad breakup with a scumbag who used her and then ruined her life. By the way, those are her words, and she was providing information I hadn't asked for."

"She probably just wanted to vent. I'm not sure if you realize it, but you have a calming way about you. People—especially women—respond to that when they're feeling frantic. What else did she say?"

"She lives in the apartment over the bar where she works and doesn't have a lot of friends, although she's joined several groups since she moved to the island in the hope of settling in and meeting people."

"You said she was on her way home from her theater group?"

Finn nodded. "She volunteers as a costume designer. It seems her true love is sewing and fashion design and she's only tending bar until she can save up enough money to go to design school. She told me that she'd dropped out of one of the best design schools in the country when her demon ex-boyfriend decided to move west and asked her to go with him. Like a fool, she gave up her dreams for a man who was destined to use and then dump her."

I raised one eyebrow. "Seems like a dramatic way of wording things."

"Again, her words, not mine. Celeste struck me as the sort who might use her looks and charm to milk whatever she could out of whatever male was closest. I don't know whether her sob story is truth or fiction, but unless this ex-boyfriend of hers turns out to be a suspect I don't think the details of her love life are relevant to the case."

"Do you think she was lying about the demon ex-boyfriend to get your sympathy?"

Finn tilted his head to one side. "I don't know. Maybe. She did suggest we could finish our interview over dinner when she's released from the hospital, but I made it clear I was very much engaged."

I smiled. "Good for you, but be forewarned: She sounds like the kind of woman who may not care if you're engaged, married, or whatever. Don't be surprised if she comes on to you again before this is over. Did she tell you anything else?"

"No. As soon as I could tell she was coming on to me I got nervous and cut the interview short."

I laughed. Finn was drop-dead gorgeous, but he'd never seemed to realize what a tempting package he brought to the table. He'd always been like another brother to me and the locals all knew he'd been Siobhan's guy since they were in high school together, but I'd witnessed many women giving him the look over the years and it took a lot for him to notice.

"Tanner was an out-of-work chef looking for a restaurant," I began, "Stuart was an out-of-work dock worker, and Celeste is a bartender with dreams of becoming a designer. I don't see any links."

"Yeah." Finn sighed. "I don't either. Without a common variable to explore we're really only left with the serial killer theory, which doesn't sit well with me at all."

"Just because we don't see a link doesn't mean one doesn't exist. At one point we thought it was the AA meeting, but we've since found out Stuart and Tanner didn't attend the same ones. There are other AA meetings on the island; I wonder if he attended a different one. If he did, the driver could be someone who floats between meetings and had the opportunity to meet both of them."

Finn rested his arms on the desk. "I interviewed several of Stuart's neighbors. They all agreed he liked to party, and as far as they could tell he wasn't doing anything to address his drinking problem. I sort of doubt he was attending AA meetings at all."

"It seems to me it might be time to revisit Siobhan's murder board. If we all brainstorm maybe we can find a link. I know you wanted us to keep a low profile, but your unwanted sidekick isn't on the island today. If we meet at Cody's there isn't any reason he'll find out we all talked."

Finn hesitated.

"And if he does find out about it, just remind him that Siobhan is my sister. We were simply getting together for dinner."

"Okay." Finn nodded. "What time?"

"I'm helping Cody get the newspaper out this morning. The storm is predicted to intensify this afternoon, so we plan to be home by then. I can text you when we're headed in that direction. You and Siobhan might want to bring an overnight bag. The peninsula road is expected to flood and you may not be able to make it back out tonight. There are plenty of extra bedrooms at Mr. Parsons's, or you can go next door to Maggie's if you'd be more comfortable there."

"I'll call Siobhan to set it up. We'll talk later."

I left Finn's office and headed next door to the newspaper. Cody had started the process of running the hard copies of the papers that would be provided to local merchants. When Orson had owned the *Madrona Island News* he'd refused to go digital and the paper almost had gone out of business, but Cody had modernized and the online edition did much better than the physical copies had ever done.

It took us several hours to print and bundle the physical copies and it would take a couple more to deliver them to the businesses that were open to receive them, but that should still get us back home by midafternoon.

"I'm going to try to get some photos for the weekend edition while we're out," Cody said. "If this storm ends up dropping the amount of rain called for it should be a newsworthy event."

"I want to stop by to check on Maggie and the cats on our way home. I'm sure they're fine, but after what happened last night…"

"No problem. I was thinking the same thing. In fact, as long as we're braving the weather why don't you call Tara to ask her if she needs anything from her place. You have a key, and now that she's settled in there might be items she's wishing she had."

I smiled at Cody. He really was the sweetest guy. Most guys I knew wouldn't give the needs of their girlfriend's best friend a second thought.

We started our route along Main Street because it was the closest to the newspaper office. Half the businesses were open, and we delivered newspapers to them, filling the racks that were displayed in front of a few others that were closed. Then we headed to Harthaven. The commercial center there was inland, as opposed to the commercial part of Pelican Bay, which was just a block off the bay. Given its location, the storm had been less intense there, and most of the businesses on Cody's list were open for the day. We decided to stop by the market to stock up on a few things should the storm linger longer than expected.

"I think I'm going to stop by the hardware store to buy the materials I'll need to fix the cat sanctuary roof when it stops raining," Cody said.

"Okay. I'll call Maggie to ask if she needs anything at the market. I wonder if Danny ever made it back to her house last night."

"With three women there, he probably stayed in town if he found someone to put him up."

"Danny has a lot of women friends who are usually willing to give him shelter for a night or two, so I doubt we'll see him until after the storm."

Cody turned into the parking lot of the hardware store. He pulled into a spot right in the front, which was good because it had started pouring rain again. He grabbed the stack of papers the store would sell for him and ran inside while I called Tara, then Maggie.

"Hi, dear. I was hoping to hear from you," Maggie greeted me.

"Cody and I are in town delivering newspapers, and then we're going to stop at the market before heading home. Do you need anything?"

"No, I stocked up when I first heard about the storm. It's been raining cats and dogs here so you'd best head back before too long or you might not make it."

"We should be home within an hour. I should probably check with Siobhan. I think she and Finn are planning to come by later."

"Siobhan called earlier and asked if they could spend the night here. I told her I was happy to have her. She did mention something about a strategy session at Cody's place."

I glanced out the window at the rain hitting the pavement. It really was getting harder. Poor Cody was going to get soaked on his way back to the truck.

"I'm afraid we're at a bit of a standstill with the investigation into Tanner's death. It never hurts to get everyone together to brainstorm. Cody's in the hardware store right now, picking up supplies to fix the roof on the cat sanctuary if it should ever stop raining. How is everyone today?"

"The cats seem to be fine. I think it was the lightning right on top of them, followed by the loud crash of the branch hitting the roof that spooked them."

"And the mama?"

"She's all settled in with her little ones and seems as content as can be. She even let me pet her today, so it seems all has been forgiven for what I had to put her through last night."

"That's good. Here comes Cody. I'll call you later, and please do call one of us if you need anything at all."

"I will, dear. And don't forget, it's best to hurry before the marsh floods and you aren't able to get back."

"We will. Love you."

I watched Cody run toward the truck with his purchases. I just hoped the rain let up a bit before we arrived at the market.

"Did you get what you need?" I asked.

"I did. I doubt I'll be able to fix the roof permanently until things dry out, but I got some temporary patch. Combined with the tarps, we should be able to keep everyone dry."

"I spoke to Maggie and she said the cats are all doing well today, including the new mom and her babies."

"That's good. Did you get hold of Tara?"

"Yeah," I confirmed. "She gave me a short list of things she needs."

"We have six stops left. Three are along this street, so we'll do them first and then we'll swing by Tara's. We'll catch the last three stops on our way to the market. As a matter of fact, the market is the last newspaper drop."

"Sounds like a plan." I glanced out the windshield. "It looks like it's letting up."

"I pulled the weather satellite map up on my phone while I was in line at the hardware store. It showed the rain letting up but the wind picking up ahead of the next system. If we hurry we can make it back before the next wave of rain hits."

We were able to make the three deliveries and get to Tara's in less than twenty minutes. She wanted a couple of things from her bedroom, where I headed, and a few others in her kitchen, where I sent Cody. Tara had a nice two-bedroom condo, where she currently lived alone. The last person to stay in the guest room had been Tanner for a couple of nights, before his memory had returned.

Everything Tara wanted was in her bedroom except for a heavy sweater, which she'd told me was in the closet of the guest room. I located the jeans, pajamas, magazines, paperbacks, and toiletries she'd asked for and placed them on her dining table before heading into the other room.

I stood at the door for a moment, pausing as I considered the shiver that worked its way up my spine. If I didn't know better I'd suspect I wasn't alone in there, but I'd already searched Tara's bedroom and the attached bath for the things I'd gathered, and I could hear Cody moving around in the kitchen, so the likelihood of there being an intruder was slim to none.

I took one step into the room and heard a scurrying noise. I paused to listen. It didn't sound like footsteps but more like someone—or probably some*thing*—running overhead. Maybe a squirrel on the roof?

I continued into the room with my senses on high alert. I thought of calling to Cody just in case there was someone hiding under the bed or even in the closet. My instincts told me to look under the bed, but the little girl inside me, who still in some ways was afraid of a monster that might lurk under the bed, decided she didn't want to know if anything or anyone was there. I continued across the room and slowly opened the closet door, then considered the contents.

There were boxes stored on the top shelf of all different shapes and sizes. I imagined many held shoes and mementos.

There were extra clothes, like the sweater Tara wanted, heavy jackets, formal dresses, and seldom-used dress clothes hanging from the rod. When I found the sweater Tara had asked for, a jacket hanging next to it slipped from its hanger and fell to the floor. I set Tara's sweater on the bed, then bent down to pick the jacket up from the floor. It appeared to be a man's jacket and certainly much too big for Tara. I was about to slip it back on the hanger when I found something in the pocket.

"Cody," I yelled so that he would hear me in the kitchen. "I found something I think you should see."

Chapter 10

Cody came running into the room. "What is it?"

"I was getting Tara's sweater and this jacket fell to the floor. I found this in the pocket." I held up a small key that looked as if it opened a lock box of some sort and a piece of paper with a series of numbers written on it. "Do you think the numbers and the key are linked?"

"I'm not sure. Bring them with you. We can ask Tara about the jacket. It might not even have belonged to Tanner."

I stuck the key and the note in my pocket and grabbed Tara's sweater. "I wonder if Finn thought to look at the personal belongings he took from Tanner's person and car."

"I'm sure he did. It would be standard procedure during any investigation. Why?"

"I don't know. I guess when I found the key I wondered if there was anything in Tanner's wallet that might tell us what it belonged to."

"Like what?" Cody found an empty box in the laundry room and began transferring everything we'd gathered into it for easier carrying.

"Like a piece of paper with a safety deposit box receipt or a locker number or something."

"You can call to ask him. I'll load all this into the truck while you do it."

Finn was out of his office when I called, but he confirmed that he'd picked up Tanner's personal belongings and they were locked up in the desk in anticipation of being sent to his next of kin. He agreed to pick them up before heading out to the peninsula so we could look through everything together.

We made the final three stops to deliver the newspapers and Cody and I headed back to his house. I hoped Finn and Siobhan would join us before too long so we could dive right into the brainstorming session we planned for the afternoon.

******

"Where do we even start?" Siobhan asked an hour later. She stood in front of the murder board, dry erase marker in hand, waiting for instructions.

"Let's make three columns and list everything we know about each victim.

Maybe we can come up with some sort of a link," I suggested.

"That seems too random," Tara said. "We already know the only link is that all three frequent bars. Tanner and Stuart both had been drinking when their accidents occurred. What about the woman?"

"She said she'd had a couple of drinks but was far from drunk," Finn answered.

"What about Tanner's personal possessions?" I asked.

Finn opened the envelope he'd brought from his office to reveal the registration for his car, an insurance card, a pen, an empty bourbon bottle, a half-empty pack of cigarettes, a matchbook from Shots, his wallet, a key chain, and a piece of paper with a hand-drawn map.

"I wonder what the map's of," Siobhan murmured.

"It looks like it might be of Harthaven Marina," I answered.

"Which is where Stuart worked," Finn added.

No one replied, but based on everyone's body language it seemed we all agreed it could be a clue.

"I brought the envelope with Stuart Evans's stuff too," Finn informed us. "Celeste Waters was released from the hospital this afternoon and her belongings were returned to her."

Finn opened the envelope of items belonging to Stuart. Inside were the registration and insurance card for his vehicle, his wallet, keys, a pen, a ticket stub from a theater in Seattle, rolling papers for hand-rolled cigarettes of some sort, and a receipt from a local liquor store.

I narrowed my gaze. "The pens. They look the same."

Finn picked up one pen and then the other. They were thick, with black handgrips and silver necks. From the materials used, they appeared to be expensive. There was no writing on the barrels, but they appeared to be, as I had suggested, exactly the same.

Cody took one and separated the two halves. "It's a tracking device. I've seen this type before."

"That must be how the driver knew where his victims would be," I realized. "I wonder who planted them."

"We're looking at high-end stuff," Cody said. "Based on my knowledge of tracking devices, the driver didn't buy these out of some online catalog. In fact, I wouldn't be a bit surprised if we find out they were originally law enforcement or even military."

Everyone paused to let that sink in.

"Did the third victim have a similar pen?" Siobhan asked.

"I'm not sure. I'll check," Finn offered.

The rest of us threw out off-the-cuff theories while Finn made his call. Could the killer be ex-military? Or even current military? There were a lot of military bases in the area; it wouldn't be unheard of for military personnel to visit the island during their time on leave.

"Ms. Waters said there was a pen matching the same description when her possessions were returned to her. She didn't know where it came from or that she even had it. She assumed it had been found in her car and might have been dropped by a passenger at one time or another."

"Okay, so now we know how the driver happened to be in exactly the right place at the right time to cause the accidents," I summarized. "Now we just need to find out who was behind the wheel of the midsized dark sedan."

"I don't know how we're supposed to figure out who the driver was based on what we have," Siobhan stated. "We don't even know if the pen was meant to track

Celeste Waters or if some passenger simply dropped it."

"What about the other items in the two envelopes?" Cody asked. "Nothing really stands out as significant, but what about the contents of their wallets?"

Stuart's wallet contained his driver's license, seven dollars, a credit card, a summons to appear in court on an outstanding warrant, and a condom. Tanner's wallet contained $223, a business card from a local real estate agent, a round-trip ticket stub for the ferry between Madrona Island and Anacortes, and a small piece of paper with a phone number on it. Finn called the number, which was answered by a woman who had a building for rent on Orcas Island. It seemed Tanner had continued to look for a space for his restaurant even after his brother-in-law had cut him off. Tara theorized that he might have had another plan to get the money he needed.

"That's odd," Tara commented after studying the stub from the ferry ticket. "Tanner told me he was sick and planned to stay at home the day he went to the mainland."

"Maybe he didn't want you to know he was leaving the island," I theorized.

"Why would he keep that from me? It's not like we were even formally dating. If he'd told me the reason he had to cancel our regular Wednesday lunch was because he had to go out of town I wouldn't have questioned it."

"Are you sure?" I asked.

Tara paused. "Okay, I guess I might have been curious and could even have asked where he was going."

"He must have been doing something he didn't want Tara to know about," Siobhan said.

Tara frowned but didn't respond.

"What about the key and the piece of paper we found at Tara's?" Cody asked.

"You found a key at my place?"

I explained about the jacket falling off the hanger when I retrieved her sweater from the guest room closet and the items I'd found in a pocket.

"The jacket was Tanner's," Tara confirmed. "I'd noticed it a week or so before the accident and intended to return it to him."

"Okay, so maybe the key is a clue."

Moirai jumped up onto my lap. He'd been quiet since he'd led me to the AA meeting. Perhaps our talk of the key was his cue to jump back into the investigation.

"Do you know what the key is for?" I asked the cat.

The group must be used to my kitty helpers because not a single person, even Finn, questioned my conversation with the cat.

"Meow." Moirai jumped off my lap and headed down the hall to Cody's bedroom. He went straight to the tackle box I'd taken from my cabin but hadn't yet had the chance to look through.

"No, the key must go to a lock. The tackle box isn't locked. I've already opened it."

"Meow." Moirai sat down in front of the box, refusing to move.

"Okay. We'll do it your way."

I picked up the tackle box and followed Moirai back down the hall to the living room, where the others were waiting. "Moirai led me to the box, although it isn't locked."

"May as well open it and see what the cat's after," Siobhan said.

I opened the box. It appeared to be filled with fishing tackle and supplies, just as I had determined the day I'd found it at Tanner's place. Siobhan suggested I unpack the box one item at a time, setting the contents on the table. If the cat showed interest in any item we'd take a closer look at it.

I unloaded the box, item by item, but the cat just sat there patiently, watching me.

"It's empty," I announced after I'd removed all the contents.

Tara got up from where she'd been sitting and joined me at the table. She began examining everything I'd removed, picking up an item, looking at it, then setting it back down before picking up another.

Moirai began pawing at the bottom of the box.

"It's empty." I held it up. "See?"

Moirai continued to paw at the box.

"Look for a false bottom," Cody said. "When I was a kid I had a tackle box with a false bottom. I hid all my treasures there."

Sure enough, I found a latch that, when pulled, exposed a key hole. I used the key I'd found in Tanner's jacket to open the bottom.

"Oh my," I gasped.

Hidden under the false bottom was cash. A lot of it. Under the cash was a piece of paper with a series of letters followed by numbers written on it. What was with all the number sequences Tanner had on scraps of paper? We'd found one in his jacket pocket and now another in the tackle box. Maybe he'd been gambling?

"I guess I should have wondered how Tanner had been paying for things," Tara admitted. "I assumed he was getting money from his ex-brother-in-law, but when Finn told us the brother-in-law had cut him off, I should have stopped to ask where he'd been getting the money he always seemed to have."

"I think the numbers on this paper," Finn said, gesturing to the one from the box, "are case numbers. The sequence is the same."

"What kind of case numbers?" I asked.

"I don't know, but I can find out." Finn looked at Cody. "Can I borrow your laptop?"

"Yeah, sure. I'll set it up on the kitchen table."

Cody and Finn worked to test Finn's theory while Siobhan and I put something together for dinner. It looked like the Scooby Gang might be working late into the night. We decided on spaghetti and garlic bread. Siobhan made the sauce while I buttered the bread and threw together a salad.

After a bit of research Finn discovered that all the case numbers on the list belonged to warrants that were currently outstanding.

"Why would Tanner want them?" Tara asked.

"Maybe he was tracking down the individuals with the outstanding warrants and blackmailing them," Siobhan suggested. "It would account for the cash."

"I suppose that's possible," Tara admitted. "Are all the outstanding warrants local?"

"No. There are some with addresses within the San Juan Islands but others where the last known address is Seattle or the outlying areas."

"What about the numbers on the paper I found in his pocket?" I wondered.

Finn looked at it. "These are different." He continued to study the paper. "They're written in short sequences of four numbers followed by six numbers, then another six. The ones with six numbers could represent dates or maybe locker combinations. I'm not sure what the sequences with four numbers could relate to."

"Maybe locker numbers or safety deposit box numbers," Siobhan suggested. "They could even be the last four digits of account numbers."

"The food's ready," I announced. "Let's eat, and then we'll pick things up again when we're done."

Siobhan rarely cooked because she was so busy, but when she did, there was a certain magic to everything she prepared. I guess some people are born with the knack, whether they choose to nurture it or not. The spaghetti sauce was absolutely perfect. It was a mostly quiet meal as everyone dug in until they couldn't eat another bite.

We did the dishes and all returned to the living room to pick up where we'd left off. Siobhan and I poured over the series of numbers, trying to make sense of them, while Cody pulled up background details on the outstanding warrants and looked at each one with Finn. Tara was feeling light-headed after the long day, so she curled up on the sofa with Bandit and Moirai and watched as the four of us worked.

"The warrants seem to span a fairly long period of issue dates and the original charges include everything from burglary to parking tickets," Finn said aloud.

"So, are we thinking one of the people Tanner was blackmailing—if that's indeed what was going on—killed him?" Siobhan asked.

"If his was the only death I might think that," Finn answered, "but I don't see how Tanner's activity led to the other targets."

"The warrants are all for nonviolent and mostly petty crimes. A lot of people skip out on their court dates. It would take a tremendous amount of manpower to track them all down. Unless the instigating crime is serious, in most cases a warrant is issued, but little else is done to find the offender."

"So what's the point of the warrant?"

"If the person is picked up for some other crime or is pulled over for speeding, the warrant will be on file and they'll have to answer to the warrant as well as the new charge. We actually do end up catching up with quite a few offenders on outstanding warrants over time."

Tara picked up the warrants Cody had printed out from the paper we'd found in Tanner's tackle box and Stuart's possessions. She studied them while Cody and Finn continued to work. If Tanner had been blackmailing the individuals with outstanding warrants he'd been a lot more skilled at detective work than we could have imagined.

"Look at these two." Tara held up the warrants she'd been studying. She handed them to Finn. "Do you notice anything curious?"

Finn squinted as he considered the two sheets of paper in front of him. He looked up with a frown on his face. "Both were issued for failure to appear in hearings relating to Drinking Under the Influence." He passed the warrants to Cody. "One warrant was for Stuart Evans and one was for Tanner Woodson. And both tickets were initially issued by Deputy Warren Strong."

"The same Deputy Strong who's been hanging around all week?" I asked.

Finn nodded. "One and the same."

"Is that relevant?" Siobhan asked.

Finn frowned. "I'm not sure."

Everyone paused to let this new information sink in. Two of the three victims of the car accidents had been wanted on outstanding warrants initially written by the very person sent to investigate the incidences.

"How about Celeste?" I asked. "Can you check to see if she has an outstanding warrant or if she's ever had a DUI?"

Finn logged back into the sheriff's database. "It looks like Celeste did have a DUI issued by the Seattle Police, but I don't see any outstanding warrants. Still, the fact that all three have DUIs and had been drinking at the time of their accidents seems relevant."

"Maybe drinking and driving made them targets," Tara offered.

"What exactly did the sheriff say to you when he called to let you know Deputy Strong would be overseeing the investigation into Tanner's accident?" Cody asked.

"I never spoke to him. Strong just showed up after Tanner's accident and told me that he'd been sent by the sheriff. I had no reason to doubt him. I know he's a fairly recent recruit for the county, but he does work out of the main office." Finn frowned again. "I need to make a phone call."

Cody and I looked at each other. "You don't think...?"

"Actually, I do." He turned back to the computer and began typing.

"Do the two of you mind filling the rest of us in on your shorthand?" Tara asked.

"It's occurred to us that Deputy Strong is the man we're after," I answered.

"Why on earth would Deputy Strong kill Tanner and the others?" Siobhan ansked. "I'm sure a lot of people he writes tickets for don't show up for their court date."

"True," I said, "but the fact that he showed up on the island at all and that his name is listed on warrants found in the possession of two of the accident victims seems too darn coincidental."

We all looked up as Finn walked back into the room. "I called the sheriff. He didn't send Deputy Strong. In fact, he said Strong left for a training class two days before Tanner was killed in the accident. He doesn't expect him back until Monday."

"So he could have already been on the island," Tara provided.

"Wait." Siobhan stepped away from the white board. "I thought Strong left on the last ferry yesterday. The third accident took place after the ferry departed."

"He said he was going home to San Juan Island, but I didn't actually see him board the ferry."

"So he could still be on the island," I stated.

"Maybe a better question is, why would Deputy Strong run people off the road?" Siobhan asked.

Cody spoke up. "I think I know." He looked up from the computer. "Deputy Strong's wife and daughter were killed by a drunk driver two years ago. He took personal leave for a while after that. When he returned to service he requested a transfer to San Juan County."

"So he requested a transfer to our county in order to have a means of running people off the road?" Tara asked. "Tanner wasn't even living here when Strong must have first arrived. I don't think Stuart was either."

"I doubt his intention at the time of the transfer was to target drunk drivers. Something must have happened to set him off," Finn theorized.

"So what now?" I asked.

"I filled the sheriff in. He's going to try to track Strong down. He'll call me back either way. Hopefully, Strong won't know we're on to him and he'll answer the sheriff's call."

"I'm going to take the dogs out," I announced.

"It's pouring rain," Siobhan reminded me.

"The dogs still need a bathroom break. I won't be long."

"Do you want me to come with you?" Cody asked.

"No. Why don't you go ahead and find out what else you can about Deputy Strong? If he doesn't get back to the sheriff we may need to track him down. I hate to think that he might still be on the island. The likelihood of his hunting his targets during the storm are slight, but if that does turn out to be what's going on, I won't feel safe until he's caught and put behind bars."

"At least you've never had a DUI," Tara pointed out.

"No. But when he was questioning me, he honed in on the fact that I admitted to having a glass of wine with dinner on the night Tanner died."

"Maybe we should check your car and purse for a pen," Siobhan said.

"I might do that." I glanced at Max. "When I get back. If dogs could cross their legs I think Max would be doing it right now."

Chapter 11

Moirai darted out the door when I opened it to let Max and Rambler out. Cats hated rain and there was a nice dry litter box for them upstairs, so I couldn't imagine what was going through the feline's mind.

"Moirai, come back here," I called into the darkness from my vantage point under the overhang from the second story of the large house. When he didn't return I ventured out into the rain only to have him dash under Cody's truck.

"Come out," I called. "It's wet and muddy. I really don't want to have to climb under the truck to get you."

The cat still wouldn't come out and I was contemplating the choice between going after him and waiting for him to come out on his own when someone grabbed me from behind. I tried to scream, but whoever had grabbed me had a firm grip on my mouth. I still couldn't see my captor, but one thing was certain: the individual who held me was very, very, strong.

"Deputy Strong," I said once he shoved me into the back of his sheriff's car, locking the door behind me. "What are you doing?"

"Do you have your phone?"

I couldn't prevent a slight glance down at my sweatshirt. "No," I lied.

He looked at the bulge in my pocket. "Hand it over."

I reached into my pocket and gave it to him. "Is there a problem?" I tried to act like I had no idea what was going on. Maybe he was just there to arrest me, not kill me.

Strong started the car and pulled away without answering. I tried several times to engage him in conversation as he drove away from the peninsula, but he totally ignored me. Finally, he pulled over to the side of the road. He still hadn't said anything, but he used my phone to look up a number and then send a text.

"Who are you texting?" I asked.

I frantically looked around as the deputy sat silently staring out the front window. We were on the side of the road near a drainage ditch that was empty except for extrahigh tides combined with heavy rain. Tonight the ditch would overflow with water rushing back to the sea. I gasped as my phone jangled to let me know I had a text. It was Danny; I had personalized sounds for all the most important people in my life.

"Why did you text my brother?"

"I told him you were broken down on the side of the road and asked him to come get you. He just confirmed that he's on his way."

"Why would you do that?" I glanced at the water filling the ditch on the side of the road. And then I knew. "You're going to run him into the ditch like you did the others."

"I wondered if you'd figured it out by now."

"But why Danny?"

"His truck has been sitting at Shots for the past two hours. You know he's been drinking. But when I texted him pretending to be you, he didn't hesitate to come for you."

"I'm his sister. What was he supposed to do?"

"Suggest you call someone else or call someone for you. There are any number of options preferable to getting behind the wheel of a car after you've been drinking."

"You don't know that he's drunk."

"Can you offer a single explanation as to what he might have been doing at

Shots for the past two hours if not drinking?"

He had me there. Drinking was the only activity going on at Shots and we both knew it.

"When he gets here why don't you just pull him over and arrest him? That seems a much better response than running him into the ditch."

He was staring at his phone but didn't answer.

"The ditch is full of water. He could drown," I insisted.

Strong turned and looked at me. "Have you ever had someone you loved more than life itself die in your arms?"

"No," I admitted.

"I have."

He got out of the car, opened the back door, and told me to get out too. I hesitated at first, but he had a gun so I did as he demanded. Then he got back into the car and pulled forward. I could see headlights in the distance. I screamed for Danny to watch out, but of course he couldn't hear me. I watched helplessly as Strong turned on his brights at the last minute and headed straight toward Danny. I ran as fast as I could as Strong straightened out his car and drove off into the rain and Danny's truck flew over the guardrail and into the water-filled ditch.

When I arrived at the place where the truck had gone in I hesitated. The water had begun to recede and the current from the storm drain to the sea was strong. Danny's truck was slowly going under, and from where I stood, I couldn't tell whether he was dead or alive, conscious or unconscious.

Finally, I waded into the water, grabbing onto tree branches and submerged shrubs as I made my way against the current toward the truck. By the time I arrived at the partially submerged vehicle only Danny's head was above the waterline.

"Danny," I screamed as loud as I could, "you have to get out."

He didn't respond. There was blood streaming from his head down his face. I still didn't know if he was dead or unconscious, but if I didn't get him out soon, *dead* was going to be the only option.

I couldn't open the door and the truck windows were electric. Strong had kept my phone so I didn't have any way to call for help. My only hope was that someone on the road would see Danny's headlights and stop to help. On any other night that would have been a real possibility, but on this dark, stormy night everyone had wisely chosen to stay in. I hadn't seen a single car on the road since Strong had left the peninsula.

The truck jerked and submerged several more feet. Another few inches and Danny's head would be below the waterline. I looked around for something to break the window. I knew the bank of the man-made ditch was lined with rocks. The question was whether I had time to get back to the bank, grab a rock, break the window, and pull Danny out before he drowned. I didn't see a better option, so I yelled to him to hang on before making my way back to the bank.

The going was slow against the strong current, but I wouldn't be able to help Danny if I was swept out to sea. I made my way from branch to branch, praying all the way. When I arrived at the bank I grabbed the largest rock I could carry with one hand and slowly made my way back to the truck. A large tree branch that must have broken off in the wind hit the side of the truck as it made its way to the sea. The force of the branch hitting the truck sent it under the rest of the way.

I knew it was now or never. I took a deep breath and dunked beneath the surface of the water. It was murky, but the truck's headlights were still on, permitting me to see what was right in front of me. Danny was completely underwater at this point and still hadn't woken up, which, I realized, wasn't a good sign. I hit the window with the rock multiple times until it shattered, then I grabbed Danny, who hadn't been wearing a seat belt, and tried to pull him out through the window. He was heavy, even in the water, so I swam to the surface for another breath before returning to the shattered window, where I grabbed onto Danny's shirt and pulled with all my might.

Somehow—I have no idea how—I managed to pull him free and bring us both to the surface. The current had gotten stronger, requiring me to hold on to my brother with both hands. Of course with both hands occupied trying to keep Danny's head above the surface, I was unable to hold on to an anchor, which meant we were both temporarily swept downstream. I had seen there was a sharp curve in the ditch before it emptied into the sea; my only hope was to make a final push toward the side, allowing the momentum of the water to carry me.

I have no doubt in my mind that some source of divine intervention was at work that night. One minute Danny and I were being swept away and the next I realized we'd been thrust up on the bank. I pulled Danny away from the moving water and began to administer CPR.

"Come on, Danny," I begged as I pumped his chest. "You can't die on me now."

I was exhausted from my time in the water and wasn't sure how long I could continue administering CPR. I was on the verge of giving up when Danny coughed up a lungful of water and took his first breath.

"Cait?" Danny said when he was finally able to breathe freely.

"It's okay. I have you," I sobbed as tears streamed down my face. I held his head and upper body in my arms and rocked him back and forth. "We're safe. I saw headlights on the road. When whoever passed by sees the lights from your truck they'll stop to investigate."

At least I hoped they would. The water in the ditch was continuing to rise with the heavy rain. It wouldn't be long before we were trapped by the steep bank and raging water.

Chapter 12

Thursday, February 9

"Why'd you let me sleep so long?" I asked Cody the next morning, or perhaps it was the next afternoon. After Danny and I had been rescued and taken to the hospital I'd insisted on waiting there to make sure he was going to be okay.

"You were tired. Your body has been through a lot. You needed to sleep."

"I wanted to go see Danny this morning. I hate to think of him being alone in the hospital. I can't imagine what he must be thinking after everything he went through."

"Siobhan stopped by earlier and picked up Tara. When they got to the hospital your mom, Cassie, and your Aunt Maggie were already visiting. I don't think Danny is in dire need of company right now."

I lay back into the softness of the pillows. It really had been a long night.

"And Deputy Strong?" I asked.

"Is in custody. Finn couldn't understand why he used his official vehicle to kidnap you rather than the dark blue sedan he'd driven to run the others off the road. He was glad he had, though, because all sheriff's vehicles are equipped with GPS and easy to find."

I was glad the man was behind bars and unable to hurt anyone else, but I did feel a little bad when I remembered the haunted look on his face as he asked me if I had ever held a loved one in my arms as they died.

"Deputy Strong told me he was there when his wife and daughter died," I informed Cody.

Cody nodded. "Finn said Strong was on duty and was the first to respond to the call after the accident. His wife was already gone, but his daughter was still alive and conscious. She was only twelve years old. I can't imagine how horrible it must have been to hold his daughter as she took her last breath. I don't condone what he's done, but I guess I can understand it."

"Yeah." I felt a tear slide down my cheek. "Me too."

Moirai jumped up onto the bed and snuggled his head under my chin as if to comfort me. I really hated the way this investigation had ended. It was easier to deal with the situation when the killer was simply evil and not someone for whom it was so easy to feel sympathy.

"I spoke to Finn," Cody informed me. "He was able to confirm that Tanner *had* been hunting down and blackmailing people with outstanding warrants. As it turned out, it was his drinking and driving and not that blackmail scheme that ended up getting him killed, but I don't think he was ever the nice guy we thought him to be."

"And the list?" I wondered.

"I'm not sure we can know for sure, but it looks like it was simply a list of people from his AA group. Again, it doesn't look like the list had anything to do with the accidents. I guess that just proves that because you find what looks to be a clue doesn't mean it actually is relevant to the case you're investigating."

I looked down at the cat. "I guess the only thing left to do is to help you get to wherever it is your journey will take you next."

"Meow."

"Can I shower and have something to eat first?"

Moirai swatted at a stray hair. He hadn't run off to the door, so I assumed it meant he was fine with waiting.

******

I showered and dressed and Cody made me a hearty breakfast. The rain had stopped and the clouds were beginning to clear. I'd called Maggie to make sure everything was okay at her place and she told me that she was still at the hospital with Danny, but he had volunteered to have a couple of his contractor friends stop by to fix the roof on the cat sanctuary.

Other than visiting Danny, I didn't have any plans for the day and wondered if I should open the bookstore. The storm had passed and the flooding had just begun to recede, so I supposed that could wait one more day. I was debating whether to go to the hospital when Siobhan called with news.

"We've set a date for the wedding," she said, an undeniable tone of joy in her voice.

"Really? When?"

"May 20."

"That's soon?"

"When Finn and I were chatting with Maggie at the hospital she told us the priest who'll be taking over for Father Kilian will be on the island by the end of the month. He'll have a few months of training before Father Kilian officially retires. At this point he's looking at the end of May or perhaps early June. Finn and I both wanted him to perform the ceremony, so we decided to jump in with both feet and do it before he leaves."

I felt like crying again, only this time they would be happy tears. Finn and Siobhan were finally getting married. "I'm so happy for you," I said.

"Thanks. I'm pretty happy myself. We decided to keep it simple. After the ceremony at St. Patrick's we'll have the reception at Maggie's. We want to keep it small, just family and friends."

"Sounds perfect."

"I think it will be perfect, as long as you agree to be my maid of honor."

My breath caught. I wasn't sure why I was so shocked, but I was. "You want me?"

"There's no one I'd rather have. So how about it? Will you stand up with me as I finally marry the only man I've ever loved?"

"Yes," I cried. "There's nothing I want more."

******

Later, I found Cody staring at Moirai, who was sleeping soundly on the sofa, having made absolutely no move on to the next stop along his way. In the past, once a mystery had been solved, Tansy's cats either had led me to their next destination or, in a few instances, their owners somehow had found us and come to pick up their missing kitty.

"Maybe this one's going to stay," Cody said.

"I wouldn't mind if he wanted to. He's a great cat. But that isn't how it's worked in the past and I sense that isn't what's supposed to happen now."

"You could call Tansy," Cody suggested. "Maybe she knows."

"I might. If he's still here tomorrow I will."

Cody looked out the window. "It's turning out to be a nice day. Do you want to take the dogs for a walk?"

"In a bit. Tara texted me a while ago. She said she's feeling a lot better and wants to move back into her own place. She's coming by soon to pick up Bandit."

"It seems the slumber party is over. Mr. Parsons told me Banjo and Summer have gone home as well."

"Personally, I'm ready for some normalcy."

"Yeah," Cody agreed. "Normal sounds pretty good about now." He glanced out the window again. "It looks like Tara's here. I can start carrying her stuff down."

When Tara arrived at the door of Cody's apartment she was with a man and a young girl who looked to be about ten.

"This is Dr. Parker Hamden," Tara introduced me to the handsome man. "I wanted to thank him for taking such good care of me so I invited him to dinner."

I couldn't help but notice the color on Tara's face which, if I had to guess, was due to the man standing beside her rather than simply her improving health.

"We met at the hospital after your accident," I said. "It's good to see you again."

"And this," Tara stepped aside, "is Amy. She's Parker's niece."

"I'm happy to meet you as well," I greeted the child, who had locked her eyes on the cat.

"Can I pet your cat?" Amy asked.

"It's fine with me. His name is Moirai."

I watched as Moirai got up from his position on the sofa and trotted over to the girl, who had dropped to her knees on the carpet.

"Amy's mother is away and her father has never been in the picture, so Parker is caring for Amy for the time being," Tara whispered to me. "She really seems taken with the cat."

"And he with her." I watched the pair interact. "I don't suppose Parker and Amy are in the market for a cat?"

Tara grabbed my arm and pulled me aside. Once we were out of earshot from the others, she explained that Amy's mother was in prison and Dr. Hamden had just been granted custody. He was still trying to settle into his new role as a single father, but a cat for Amy might be just the thing. I told Tara I'd check with Tansy just to be sure Moirai didn't belong to anyone else, and Tara said she'd speak with Parker to be sure he was willing to adopt a cat, but if my intuition was correct, not only would Amy have a new cat and Moirai a new human, Tara would have a new guy in her life as well.

Life was unpredictable, consisting of highs and lows, new beginnings and difficult endings. There were secrets to be kept and revealed, as well as challenges to conquer and others we couldn't surmount and eventually must surrender to.

If there was one thing I'd found to be true in the past years, it was that the reality we experienced each day was a temporary state that would inevitably give way to a new paradigm. As our lives evolved, we drew strength from those closest to us and, as time passed, we said good-bye to some and welcomed others destined to join us on our life's journey.

As I watched Tara with Parker and Amy, I silently bid farewell to Tanner and offered a warm welcome to the new people I instinctively knew would become part of my tribe.

New Series by Kathi Daley Book

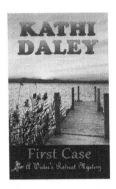

Coming in March 2017

Recipes

Recipes from Kathi
Ground Beef Stroganoff
Scalloped Ham and Potato Casserole
Chicken and Rice
Chicken Tortilla Casserole

Recipes from Readers
Breakfast Casserole—submitted by Martie Peck
Hunter's Stew—submitted by Nancy Farris
Beef à la Flo—submitted by Jeannie Daniel
A Taste of Mexico Chicken Casserole—submitted by Vivian Shane

Ground Beef Stroganoff

Brown 1 lb. of ground beef

Add 4 cloves of garlic, chopped.
Add ½ onion, chopped.
Salt and pepper to taste.

When meat is brown, add:
16 oz. sour cream
5 cups sliced mushrooms
4 oz. cream cheese
½ cup soy sauce
½ cup grated Parmesan cheese

Simmer until warm and well blended.

Serve over wide egg noodles.

Scalloped Ham and Potato Casserole

5–6 large potatoes, peeled and thinly sliced
2 cups cooked ham, cubed
1 cup grated cheddar cheese

Sauce:

Melt 1 stick butter (real butter, no substitutions) in saucepan over medium heat.
When melted add:

½ 8-oz. pkg. cream cheese
2 cups heavy whipping cream

Stir until cream cheese is completely dissolved.

Slowly add:

2 cups grated Parmesan cheese (the good stuff)
1 cup grated Romano cheese (add slowly; don't let it clump)

Stir until smooth.

Add:

1 tsp. ground nutmeg
½ tsp. garlic powder
Salt and pepper to taste

Layer half potatoes, ham, and sauce in greased deep casserole dish. Repeat. Top with cheddar cheese.

Cook at 400 degrees for 45 minutes or until potatoes are tender.

Chicken and Rice

Traditional

Combine:

1½ cups Minute rice
2 cans mushroom soup
2 soup cans milk
2 packets onion soup mix

Pour into greased 9 x 13 baking dish.
Place 3–4 chicken breasts on top. Cover with foil.
Bake for 60 minutes at 350 degrees.

Remove foil and bake uncovered for an additional 20 minutes.

Cheesy chicken and rice

Combine:

1½ cups Minute rice
1 can cheddar cheese soup
1 jar Alfredo sauce
1 soup can milk

Pour into greased 9 x 13 baking dish.
Place 3–4 chicken breasts on top. Cover
with foil.
Bake for 60 minutes at 350 degrees.

Remove foil and bake uncovered for an
additional 20 minutes.

Note: Sometimes I spread shredded
cheddar over the top after I remove the
foil.

Chicken Tortilla Casserole

4 chicken breasts, cooked and cubed
2 cans (7 oz.) diced green chilis
1 can (10 oz.) chicken broth
1 can (10 oz.) cream of mushroom soup
1 can (10 oz.) cream of chicken soup
1 large can or 2 small cans sliced black olives
1 can (15 oz.) corn, drained

Combine everything above and set aside.

1 pkg. corn tortillas
2 cups shredded cheddar cheese

Layer half of tortillas, half of soup, and half of cheese in greased 9 x 13 baking pan.

Repeat with second half.

Bake at 350 degrees for 30 minutes.

Breakfast Casserole

Submitted by Martie Peck

I make this casserole for every holiday get-together. Fruit salad, English muffins, fresh OJ, and coffee round out our brunch. You start this casserole the night before with dried, day-old bread.

4 cups cubed day-old, firm, dried-out white or French bread
2 cups or 8 oz. shredded cheddar cheese
10 eggs, lightly beaten
4 cups milk
1 tsp. dry mustard
1 tsp. salt
¼ tsp. onion powder
Dash fresh ground pepper
1 lb. Italian sausage, cooked (I use Bob Evans)
Fresh mushrooms (optional)

Spray cooking spray in a 9 x 11 baking pan, arrange bread cubes in dish, and sprinkle with cheese. Beat together the next 5 ingredients, pepper to taste. Pour evenly over bread. Sprinkle with cooked sausage and optional mushrooms. Cover with foil and refrigerate overnight. In the morning preheat oven to 325 degrees, bake uncovered until set, about 1 hour. If top gets too brown put foil tent over casserole.

Because half my family doesn't like mushrooms I only put them on half of the casserole.
This tastes great reheated in the microwave the next day—if there's any left over.

Hunter's Stew

Submitted by Nancy Farris

This is one of our favorite cold-weather meals, plus the leftovers are wonderful! You can use a venison roast instead of beef if there's a hunter in the family.

Serves 6

1 tbs. olive oil
1½ lbs. chuck roast
Salt and pepper
2 cups beef broth
¾ cup dry red wine
1 bay leaf

1 cup wild rice
2 tbs. olive oil
1 medium onion, chopped
2 carrots, chopped
1 rib celery, chopped
1 clove garlic, chopped
6 cups beef broth
Salt and pepper

Preheat the oven to 300 degrees. In large oven-proof pan, heat olive oil. Season the roast with salt and pepper to taste. Cook over high heat until browned, about 2 minutes per side. Add the 2 cups of beef broth and wine and bring to simmer. Add bay leaf. Cover and braise in the oven for 2–2½ hours until tender. I normally turn it over about halfway through cooking.

Meanwhile, heat an enameled saucepan over high heat. Add the wild rice and stir until it starts to pop, about 2 minutes. Add the 2 tbs. olive oil and the onion, carrots, celery, and garlic and stir for 2 more minutes. Add the 6 cups of beef broth and bring to simmer. Cover and cook about 50 minutes until the rice is tender.

Remove the meat from the broth and shred it. Put back in broth and add the cooked wild rice mixture. Simmer for 5 minutes on the stovetop and season to taste.

Serve in bowls with crusty bread. Enjoy!

Beef à la Flo

Submitted by Jeannie Daniel

My sister's mother-in-law gave her this recipe when she first married my brother-in-law over fifty years ago. It's a family favorite.

3 lbs. lean beef cubes
½ lb. beef suet or butter
3 tbs. flour
1½ tsp. salt
½ tsp. pepper
½ tsp. thyme
1 can beef broth (I like to use beef consommé for a richer, thicker sauce)
1 cup dry red wine
½ lb. fresh mushrooms
1 onion, chopped

Sauté cubes in the fat, stir in flour, salt, pepper, and thyme. Scrape the skillet for all the good bits and add broth and wine. Cook for 2 hours. Add the mushrooms and onions and cook for 90 minutes. Skim the fat from the top of the gravy. I make mine in a black iron Dutch oven. This can be put over noodles or mashed potatoes or eaten alone.

A Taste of Mexico Chicken Casserole

Submitted by Vivian Shane

One of those old-time casseroles that just tastes good on a cold night!

½ cup chopped onion
½ cup chopped celery
1 tsp. butter
1 can cream of chicken soup
1 can golden mushroom soup
1 8-oz. can diced tomatoes
1 4-oz. can chopped green chilies
1 doz. corn tortillas
2 cups cooked chicken
¼ lb. grated cheddar cheese

Sauté onion and celery in butter until tender. Add soups, tomatoes, and chilies and heat through. Spray 9 x 13 pan with vegetable spray and line with 3 corn tortillas. Place ⅓ chicken, ⅓ soup, and ⅓ cheese on top of tortillas. Repeat layers two more times. Bake at 350 degrees for 30 minutes.

Books by Kathi Daley

Come for the murder, stay for the romance.

Zoe Donovan Cozy Mystery:

Halloween Hijinks
The Trouble With Turkeys
Christmas Crazy
Cupid's Curse
Big Bunny Bump-off
Beach Blanket Barbie
Maui Madness
Derby Divas
Haunted Hamlet
Turkeys, Tuxes, and Tabbies
Christmas Cozy
Alaskan Alliance
Matrimony Meltdown
Soul Surrender
Heavenly Honeymoon
Hopscotch Homicide
Ghostly Graveyard
Santa Sleuth
Shamrock Shenanigans
Kitten Kaboodle

Costume Catastrophe
Candy Cane Caper
Holiday Hangover
Easter Escapade – *April 2017*

Zimmerman Academy The New Normal
Ashton Falls Cozy Cookbook

Tj Jensen Paradise Lake Mysteries by Henery Press

Pumpkins in Paradise
Snowmen in Paradise
Bikinis in Paradise
Christmas in Paradise
Puppies in Paradise
Halloween in Paradise
Treasure in Paradise – *April 2017*
Fireworks in Paradise – *October 2017*

Whales and Tails Cozy Mystery:

Romeow and Juliet
The Mad Catter
Grimm's Furry Tail
Much Ado About Felines
Legend of Tabby Hollow
Cat of Christmas Past
A Tale of Two Tabbies
The Great Catsby
Count Catula
The Cat of Christmas Present
A Winter's Tail
The Taming of the Tabby – *May 2017*

Seacliff High Mystery:

The Secret
The Curse
The Relic
The Conspiracy
The Grudge

Sand and Sea Hawaiian Mystery:

Murder at Dolphin Bay
Murder at Sunrise Beach
Murder at the Witching Hour
Murder at Christmas

Murder at Turtle Cove – *March 2017*

Road to Christmas Romance:
Road to Christmas Past

Writer's Retreat Southern Mystery:
First Case – *May 2017*
Second Look – *July 2017*

Kathi Daley lives with her husband, kids, grandkids, and Bernese mountain dogs in beautiful Lake Tahoe. When she isn't writing, she likes to read (preferably at the beach or by the fire), cook (preferably something with chocolate or cheese), and garden (planting and planning, not weeding). She also enjoys spending time on the water when she's not hiking, biking, or snowshoeing the miles of desolate trails surrounding her home.

Kathi uses the mountain setting in which she lives, along with the animals (wild and domestic) that share her home, as inspiration for her cozy mysteries.
Kathi is a top 100 mystery writer for Amazon and won the 2014 award for both Best Cozy Mystery Author and Best Cozy Mystery Series.

She currently writes six series: Zoe Donovan Cozy Mysteries, Whales and Tails Island Mysteries, Sand and Sea Hawaiian Mysteries, Tj Jensen Paradise Lake Mysteries, Writer's Retreat Southern Mysery, and Seacliff High Teen Mysteries.

Giveaway:

I do a giveaway for books, swag, and gift cards every week in my newsletter, *The Daley Weekly* http://eepurl.com/NRPDf

Other links to check out:

Kathi Daley Blog – publishes each Friday
http://kathidaleyblog.com

Webpage – www.kathidaley.com

Facebook at Kathi Daley Books –
www.facebook.com/kathidaleybooks

Kathi Daley Books Group Page –
https://www.facebook.com/groups/569578823146850/

E-mail – kathidaley@kathidaley.com

Twitter at Kathi Daley@kathidaley –
https://twitter.com/kathidaley

Amazon Author Page –
https://www.amazon.com/author/kathidaley

BookBub –
https://www.bookbub.com/authors/kathi-daley

Pinterest – http://www.pinterest.com/kathidaley/

Made in the USA
San Bernardino, CA
17 June 2018